CW01213540

# MISSING

## BY

## SHIREEN JABRY

*Enjoy the read!*

*lots of love from*

© 2013 Lulu Author. All rights reserved.

ISBN

*Things are not always what they seem*

"Come on George!" She was yanking my sleeve, pestering me to follow her.

"Julia, let go of me," said George with a smirk on his face.

"No way hose."

"Give it to me now or die trying…"

She smiled mischievously at me, almost begging me to give her my only treasure that I had been collecting since my early wee years.

"Let it go, Jules," said George. "There is no other way around this."

George's words were final.

But Jules had other things in store for him.

Letting go of her grip, she suddenly jumps up and runs in the opposite direction, leaving a surprised George behind.

## **Chapter ONE**

"Suck it up! Suck it up, man!"

"You need to …."

"I know, I know, to suck it up as you keep on saying over and over again."

"Forget her."

That was Jason, as forgetful as they come. It was like he had a DVD memory that only kicked in when he ordered it to. He pressed pause and things just drew to a close in his life and eject when he had enough of watching the same thing, over and over again. Now he was busy telling me to eject her – right out of my life.

"Come on, all she did is steal your shit."

"Can you please stop saying that?"

"Saying what?"

"You know what I'm talking about."

George was serious, so serious that his bad mood was all her doing.

"Look man, I just want my …"

"I know what you want, forget it, she got the better of you and took your Comic, granted it's a special edition of the Hulk and …."

"It's an antique edition."

I looked at him and at once my eyes began to tear up.

"Now don't go doing that."

"Girls do that."

"Stop it man."

I cried silently, as the tears rolled down my face, my back remained turned in the face of my buddy, Jase.

He walked over to me and patted my back.

"Girls are pains in the neck man. Just get used to it, easiest way to deal with it, just get used to it."

As an afterthought he added, "That's why we're here."

"We're men, real men," he said as he emphasized the 'real' word, pronouncing it with all the force he could muster.

### George's Description:

*A tall thin boy with brown hair and little brown ruffles that get into the way of his eyes every now and then. Hazel eyes and a fair colored white skin tone embraces the features of this charming boy.*

### Chapter TWO

"Wake up man and stop snoring already."

Jase was over at George's bedroom trying to get him psyched.

"Okayyy," said George as he rolled over to his side ignoring his friend.

"Come on, come on, come on, come on, come on," he nagged repeatedly.

George pushed himself up on the bed and rubbed his eyes, opening them to see Jase blurry and impatient as always.

Jase holds up a torch of light and shines it in George's eyes.

Then he grabs the torch, turning it on himself and lights up his face in the midst of darkness.

"Sleep-over time."

And with that comment he switches off the torch, gets out of bed and walks to the en-suite bathroom.

A half an hour later and George is standing in front of his bathroom door growing irritable in minutes.

"HALO? What the heck are you doing in there?"

He rests his ear against the door, hoping to hear a reply.

But he hears nothing.

"Okay man, stop pulling my leg, you win, just come out here already, I promise I won't nag about Jules and the Comic that she stole."

Even as he said it, he could tell his promise is hollow and he's lying.

"I know that doesn't sound too convincing but honestly I won't mention it, not tonight anyway."

He starts knocking slowly on the door, being careful not to knock too hard and wake up his parents downstairs in the middle of their sleep.

He didn't need to be grounded AGAIN.

Last week was more than enough to last him a lifetime.

But still - nothing.

He presses his ear to the door and listens hard.

Timmy wakes up and walks right behind George and his ears prick up the sound of gushing water.

He barks a mellow little bark, as if he knows the time of the night and is making sure that George doesn't get grounded by his parents for what would seem like the millionth time already this year.

At the sound of his bark, George turns around and bends down to Timmy as he pats the dog on the head and hugs him warmly as he always does every morning and every night before he goes to bed.

Timmy already started to make him feel a whole lot better.

He still had no idea about his friend but with Timmy by his side, he knew then that no other friend really mattered.

"Timmy, do you think he's washing up but it's been like 45 minutes already."

Timmy just nods in answer to his question.

George leans against the bathroom door, his back to the door and Timmy jumps eagerly into his lap as always. George awakes the next morning with Timmy licking his face.

"Oh what happened, Timmy?" he asks him as he wakes up properly after a full night's sleep.

As he gets up, he grudgingly looks at his watch.

He yawns when he sees that it's only 9 am on a Sunday morning.

He turns expecting to find Jase in his bed, sleeping away the seconds that give way to minutes which give way to hours.

But all that he finds is the ruffled bed sheets on his side of the bed.

"I'm going to kick his ass, this has gone far enough," says George to no one in particular.

### *Jason's Description:*

*He is short, chubby with a tendency to shave his dirty blonde hair every once in a while trying to recreate his look. It's hard to figure out his main hair look that keeps on changing at a whim, but at this point in time, his hair is marine cut – shaved and his eyes curious as hell scatter around looking at everything and everyone, are dark brown.*

*Tanned and cheeky he attracts quite a lot of girls easily.*

## **Chapter THREE**

"Jules stop messing around, I'm being serious here."

"George you know how Jase is, he just loves doing this kind of stuff."

"No but this time it's out of his character."

As an afterthought he adds, "Trust me on this Jules."

"What does Timmy think?"

"Well, he was barking when he heard the sound of water coming from the bathroom."

"Yeah but then again, doesn't he always bark at sounds like that?"

She had a point, although he didn't want to admit it.

Timmy was intelligent, the best dog a man could ever have.

"No, you know how smart Timmy is," he stated convincingly.

"Smart is one thing but I don't know."

She sits down in front of him facing the fresh waters of the lake just outside the outskirts of the suburbs.

It has been their favorite place since they were kids – since they were 8 years old. George and Jules used to come up here in the weekends.

"It took us 30 minutes to get here by car and your parents are a little pissed with us, so let's make this worth it."

He turned to her and the picture of surprise bit into his features.

"You think it's not worth it to be here now, together," he croaked feeling a little pain creep into his chest like the slanting of the morning light at sun rise.

The minute she notices his face, she hugs him long and hard and when she pulls back and looks into his face she sees the old chirpy George staring back at her.

"So what now?" she asks not knowing why she was asking one thing but meaning something else entirely.

"Now, well now, we wait I guess."

"You're guessing, really?"

She is not sure why that disappoints her so much.

But she knows one thing that it's not about Jase although George is only talking about Jase.

"Let's take a walk," he says as he smiles at her.

"Be careful but it sounds like the next thing out of your mouth will be let's get coffee with that."

"Yuck that bitter stuff." And just like that George was a boy all over again and Jules a girl on the verge of womanhood, although she wasn't aware of it yet, truth be told none of them were.

### Julia's Description:

*She is neither tall nor short of medium height and small build. Of average weight, she dresses in a manner that allows her to express her creativity, her hair is full bodied and jet black in color and her eyes are the darkest brown almost black framed with a whiter than white skin tone that she dislikes and keeps on trying to tan and turn into a shade of golden brown.*

### Chapter FOUR

"Timmmmmmy!" "Tiiiiiimmmmmyyy!"

I heard Jules calling off into the distance and my heart somersaulted to my feet.

I hurried up in the toilet with a well of fear growing in my gut.

I opened the door and ran straight into my aunt.

"Sweetheart, watch out you'll trip this way," said his aunt as she gently scolded him.

"Auntie not now…"

I shoved her gently out of the way and ran on outside to Jules side.

"Hi George," she calmed down the minute she set eyes on me.

"What's wrong with Timmy?" I asked her.

I dared not ask the next question.

"Don't worry Georgie, he just went round the woods to get a twig and is not back yet."

I jolted running after him into the woods as Jules ran after me.

"Timmmmyyyyy, where are you!?"

Jules caught up with me and said, "What's wrong? He always disappears in the woods after some twig and gets back later."

"I know but look what happened to Jase, we don't even know where he is."

I said calmly.

"Listen, listen to me, Jase is messing around with you, with us, Timmy is just doing what he always does, don't read into things like that."

He heaves in a sigh of relief and sits down on the shrubs and grass that form part of the woods.

"There's something that you don't know about and I need to tell you." He speaks in even tones.

"Okay," she says as curiosity starts getting the best of her.

"Tell me what is it?"

"I don't know how to quite say this but I think it's my fault that Jase has disappeared."

"How the fuck did you gather that?"

He stared at her knowing very well that she only used the 'F' word when she was blindly shocked or just about to be blindly shocked.

"Well when he was in the bathroom the other night and I was playing with Timmy……"

"Yeah?"

"What happened, Georgie?"

"Well I kind of thought to myself, I didn't say it out loud, but who needs Jase if I have Timmy…" his voice wonders off and his face lies in his hands as he tries to take back the time that he thought such evil thoughts that may have gotten his friend wiped off the face of the earth.

She held his face in her hands and said to him, "Don't be silly Georgie, you'll see, soon Jase will come back and tease all of us all over again. This is just a prank. You'll see."

"And if it's not?"

For the first time, Jules thought of the worst possible scenario and looked away from his eyes because had she continued looking at him, he may have seen her doubts as they cast a cloudy disconcerting look over her face.

George threw a twig in the direction of the woods secretly praying that both Timmy and Jase were not missing. Nobody knew their whereabouts. And for the last two days, nobody knew Jase's whereabouts either.

He wondered what that all meant.

She wondered if Jase had it in him to be such a prick to extend a prank over two days. She couldn't bring herself to continue thinking of the worst and so got up and dusted a few leaves of her lap and demanded that George do the same.

"You know what we need the most now?"

They both answered in unity, "Strawberry and banana milkshakes!"

That was the sound of two friends, the sound of two voices, the sound of two souls in sync.

### *Timothy's Description:*

*Timothy the dog is a large sized dog that is full of energy and fun loving. His hair is as long as it can get creating a cozy white snowflake look. People not the kids, call him 'snow' and he has small black beady eyes that his white fluffs of hair hide discreetly from view.*

## **Chapter FIVE**

It's the 3$^{rd}$ day that Jase remains missing and only the 1$^{st}$ that Timmy is.

But already the disappearance of both of his closest and dearest friends had taken their toll over George.

Some may say that they took their toll over Julia too.

Those two became like two peas in a pod.

Maybe in the face of tragedy, or what appeared to be possible tragedy, they had found each other.

But one has to wonder what God was doing in his spare time.

He closed a large door and opened in its place a narrow excuse for a window; almost a sorry excuse for a window.

His dad and her mum, all were genuinely concerned and rightly so.

George was having a really tough time sleeping lately since his friend's disappearance.

Every time he came close to falling asleep, he woke himself up remembering the last thing his friend had told him - *"Sleep-over time."* And that would keep him up the whole night. Then he would get up, out of bed and walk to his bathroom, close the door and lie back, leaning on the bathroom door. And that's how he slept; he could only sleep in that way.

The worst part of all of this wasn't the sleep he lost or the anxiety that would creep up on him in the darkness and stay gripping his whole nervous system until the next morning, the worst part was not having Timmy there for him, in his time of need.

"That's got to be the worst thing of all," he murmurs out loud to himself the next day in the kitchen as he sits on the table and to no one in particular.

"What's that sweetheart?" asks his aunt as she hears him and jumps to her feet in concern.

It's pretty amazing that she doesn't have the squad jumping to their feet every second that he groans or moans. Her exaggeration of his feelings and the situation was slowly driving him mad, nearly bonkers.

"Nothing," he said to her quietly not in the mood for playing the thousand and one questions game.

"Not today," he said both to his aunt and himself as he was begging his brain to take a break from all this mess that had been occupying his thoughts since day 1, since it happened.

"Where are you going, sweetheart?"

"No-where."

And with that he left the room and walked on outside to get a much deserved fresh breath of air and almost as an after-thought walked back in to call Jules; only Jules knew what he was going through after all she was going through it herself too.

How's that for a recipe for disaster?

## **Chapter SIX**

"It's been 6 days, 5 bloody lousy no sleep nights."

"Georgie, I can't sleep either."

"What do we do Jules?"

He was asking her something she couldn't possibly answer.

"Have you ever thought that if it's that easy for both Jase and Timmy to go missing, then we could go missing just as easily next?"

"Wow, I have to stop you right there."

She came and sat next to him, they were off the phone line and back on his kitchen table again.

She held both of his hands and looked into his eyes.

"We won't be going anywhere unless we choose to, that I can promise you."

"How?"

"What?"

"How can you promise me that?"

"Just leave it to me."

Her last statement relieved the pressure that had been building up since Jason's disappearance.

It's in that moment that he noticed his attachment to her. She simply made it all better, she's the sunshine in the dim parts of his life and although that realization made him feel rather overwhelmed, he was grateful for it.

Bringing him out of his reverie, she said, "You okay now?" She asked with tenderness in her voice and a compassionate tone.

He answered, "Even if I'm not completely okay just now, I know I will be.."

And looking at her he made a promise to her that he knew that he couldn't keep no matter how hard he tries.

"Soon."

She smiles, an easy smile filled with gratitude that she's finally a somebody to someone.

## Chapter SEVEN

He woke up the next morning shocked that he had slept a night finally, but even more shocked that he had spent the night crying his eyes out while still asleep.

His right cheek was drenched with tears and creased with emotions that had passed in the eerie hours of the morning but somehow he felt alive, more alive than he had in days.

He called to hear Jules voice that morning. Instead he got a blubbering, crying hysterical mum on the phone.

"Hi – Geor—and she cried in mid sentence. Jules is missing too."

And with that he dropped the handset and sent it crashing on the floor of his bedroom and ran down the stairs and outside the house, all the while running to Jules house in his pj's and no slippers to coat his rough embittered soles that were as embittered as the soul of his heart.

## Chapter EIGHT

As he ran up the stairs to the front of her house, Timmy suddenly barked loudly and in excitement stopped him dead in his tracks. George turned around and saw Timmy run straight into him as he knocked him down on his back and jumped on him licking his face with so much excitement at seeing him again.

He must have missed him almost as much as George missed him. It was a bond unlike any other, unique in ways that most people seldom understood.

"Timmy, where were you all this time?"

He screamed at Timmy but at the same time praying to God for answering at least one of his prayers and pleading with him to answer the rest.

Then a cloud in the sky above his head as Timmy was licking him, reminded him of the tragedy that would lurk behind the door of this house; namely Jules's house.

And with all the energy he had in him, all the energy of a 12 and a half year old boy, he got up, patted Timmy and let him know why he had to wait outside and that he had no idea when he'd be back for him to walk the walk back home together.

Timmy understood him and bid him farewell. It was like they had their own private language that only the dog and he understood. All his friends loved Timmy but Timmy refused to share that language with any of them, he simply refused to share that special bond with anyone but him. That made Georgie both proud and happy.

George got up enough courage and as hope started refilling the darkest arteries of his heart, he walked into the house and saw her mother in a prayer with the town's priest leading the sermon.

The priest uninterrupted with his sermon signaled for Georgie to join them. But Georgie had his own issues with God and they were not pretty.

So the priest wanted him to pray for forgiveness for his sins as Jules's mum is doing now in front of him, pray for forgiveness when God himself had committed the biggest sin of all, sins of all: Jason & Jules's disappearance?

I mean how does that work?

He must have asked that question a little too loud because:

The priest answered by finally interrupting the sermon and walking George to Jules mum were he explained in as simple as possible the terms and conditions of the prayer.

"You try it," Jules mum pleaded in tears.

And because she was going through her own form of hell, he relented and did as she wanted him too; he prayed out loud even.

"Please god, if you can grant me one thing, please bring back Jules and Jason unscathed and unhurt and untouched and safe, please god, please….."

In that second, in walks Jules, looking rather petrified at the living room that had been turned into a church right in the middle of her house.

"What the f---?" she asked looking bewildered.

Jules's mum runs to her screaming as her arms wrap tightly around her daughter almost squeezing her to death.

There is such a thing as loving someone to death and as George welcomes God back into his heart, he finally understands the reason that she had disappeared and that's to help him realize how much he loves and values her.

Not in the brother-sister kind of way or the best friend kind of way either but in the – 'I want you to be my girlfriend' kind of way.

### Martha's (Julia's mum) Description:

*She's tall and thin with a model body and look. Her hair mid-length and blonde reaches her shoulders and her eyes light blue in color resemble a peaceful sky that lights up any room she enters. Her freckles that she hates just add to her alluring beauty.*

### Chapter NINE

"What's wrong with you guys?"

"Can't a girl lose track of time and fall asleep by the lake without the whole house going up in flames?"

Her mum suddenly pulls back and the priest jumps in to her rescue.

"Flames?" they all ask at once.

"Oh, I meant in prayer."

She said rather quietly.

"The whole house going up in prayer." She assured herself and everyone around her that she was only thinking of this now, nothing more and nothing less.

"Georgie, where are your shoes and why are you in your pj's?"

She asked an innocent question that brought everybody back from the near hit tragedy that day, on an early morning at 10 am, March 14th 2013.

## Chapter TEN

I WALKED BACK home that day, Timmy by my side strolling in and out of bushes until he found a little area to do his business.

I walked back home that day with more wear and tear on the soles of my feet, but my real soul was walking right by my side, well on the left hand side of me, because the right hand side will always belong to Timmy, my dog.

Jules is walking on my left hand side and busy babbling on about her experience last night and how she had fallen asleep after so many nights since

Jason's disappearance and her shock that it suddenly happened outside in nature's greatest landscape; the lake.

I knew that something had been relight that morning, I guess you'd call it faith, faith that resembles the image of a god that brought back Jules and that must be in the process of bringing back Jase too.

Of course he first brought back Timmy, my dog. I never told you his real name – 'Timothy.'

## **Chapter ELEVEN**

But do you really care about Timmy? About his real name, isn't his nickname enough for you? I guess you want a real special relationship like the one that I have with him, right?

Well, I don't blame you.

Don't worry my friends wouldn't either.

Even if you're an adult, I can still introduce you to Timmy but usually Timmy prefers the company of kids but it may be pushing it a little if I bring him adult friends but then again as the saying goes: "There's always a first time for everything!"

I mean look at me now, Timmy, Timothy disappeared and it looks like god brought him back to me but then in the same breath tried to trick me into believing that Jules disappeared TOO, how inconsiderate!

But then again God is God and as long as we live on this earth, his rules dictate our lives, our societies and our parents. At least there is some being that is greater in authority than parents! God controls them in as much a way as they control us.

Wouldn't you say?

Let's also ask my Timmy, "What do ya think Timmy?"

He's wagging his tail repeatedly, I guess he agrees that parents need God to be their authority figure and I do too and I would go as far as saying you would too.

## Chapter TWELVE

A good 10 days after Jason's disappearance we all put up posters all over town that say the following:

Have you seen this boy?

(A picture of Jase here – ZOOMED in on his face).

Please contact his parents **+001 315 454 679** or alternatively contact Sheriff Don at Maritimes' Local Police Station on **+001 315 456 223**.

Sheriff Don, medium built and with heavy dark and hairy eyebrows was not happy that the parent's cell number was given on the flyer. He went on about it saying that it's interfering with the police investigation.

It's a police investigation now, but me and Jules, sorry I mean, Jules and I are trying our best to keep the faith against all odds. And I know the odds are taking over now and ruling but we still want to keep a little hope and faith that everything will fall into place as it should be and as it always does.

And I hope you do too.

I know it's tough, there isn't anything harder but I really hope you do. Timmy is, so should u.

### Sheriff Don's Description:

*He's a large over-weight man with a bald head and light brown eyes that look like milk chocolate. His face is tanned with a trimmed goatee and his cheeks remain red most days. He wears the same jeans over and over again but in fact he buys 5 pieces of the same item so that he can wear it continuously without much effort, his shirts that he insists on wearing daily are of three main colors: navy blue, dark brown and olive green.*

*White plain t-shirts are a must when he changes from shirts.*

## Chapter THIRTEEN

Jason's parents are another thing altogether.

They are cut up and hurt; dad and Jules's mum won't talk to us about it. We just heard in the town that his parents are seeing a daily therapist to help with losing their son to 'unknown circumstances & unknown causes.'

I'm beginning and you should know, must know that I'm beginning to get pissy again with God – sorry God but I get to see the mess of your ways in the pain and anguish on Jason's parents faces every other day in my small suburban town.

Try looking into their eyes and faces; it's so hard to ignore all that pain. You should work on your ways and of course cleaning up your mess would be an added advantage.

Sorry God to use this tone with you but you really should.

There is a knock at the door and Jules opens the door to my house and Sherriff Don is standing there.

"Can I come in kids?"

Calling us kids?

I almost wish that Jules could have slammed the door in his face for that but of course I say nothing; I am a little bit diplomatic after all.

He stands there like a jerk on caffeine as he's busy overdosing on more caffeine.

What a smart ass!

## Chapter FOURTEEN

I turn immediately and without realizing what I'm doing I yank Jules in and slam the door in the face of the Sheriff.

"Are you nuts?! Georgie, what are you thinking?" she yelled at me her face twisted in a scornful frown.

She walks over to me, holds my shoulders and starts shaking me back and forth with a violent shake.

"He's meant to find Jase! How could you do that?"

She's upset alright and I've never seen her look at me with daggers in her eyes. I start fidgeting on my left foot and look away from her.

I sit down on the beige sofa and fall back into its comfortable nest. I feel like the sofa is nesting me in its warmth and coziness.

I immediately think of Timmy.

He would know what to do next. Shame he's not here but out playing in the back yard. That's exactly when I look up and notice him running around outside, having fun and barking incessantly in the yard.

Looking at him I know I'm going to be safe.

I stand up and tell Jules what I've always known since the night Jase disappeared but have been too afraid to mouth it into words.

"Who needs Don?"

"Sheriff Don," she snaps at me.

"We have each other," I say it like it's the most obvious thing and the wisest decision I've ever made since I've been in diapers.

She stares at me – just simply stares at me.

## Chapter FIFTEEN

"Open the damn door! Open this instant, I'm ordering you! This is not a game, kiddddsss!" the Sheriff's voice shakes with anger as he knocks the front door with his fist.

Jules hurries over to the door, opens it and with one swoop of her right arm, apologizes and swings the door shut in the Sheriff's face once more!

She runs into me, it's as if she's trying to bulldoze me to the ground but in a last minute attempt – reconsiders and hugs me instead.

I'm taken aback – Jules is really a tough cookie to crack. I never can tell what she's going to do next but then again that's never fun – predicting things can be soooo boring. And she's nothing like that.

She pulls back from the hug and says to me in a little quivering voice, "We will find Jase, right?"

Her eyes start to well up with tears n fears and as the first tear gently falls onto her face and pours down the rest of her beautifully structured features, I make a promise that I'll find Jase even if it kills me first.

"I promise you, next time he will be here with us."

Suddenly she turns around and runs upstairs.

A couple of minutes later, she's downstairs again. She opens her hot pink notebook and hands me a pen.

"Let's come up with a plan."

She sounds rather relieved. I think she also didn't trust this Sheriff Don either.

I mean who did? Except adults, of course.

I write down on top of the lined paper a subheading that reads:

The Mission, crossed it out and corrected it to =

Our Mission

We bring our heads together and think long and hard.

"It's going to be an adventure alright!" she chirped.

"We are going to find Jase and rescue him and that's all there is to it! We will show that Sheriff Don! We will show him!" she sang at the top of her voice, singing it like a national anthem.

"Its payback time!" we both said at once and fell back on the sofa chuckling.

I turn to Jules, "Do you know that Don Man got me grounded for slamming that door in his face the other day."

"Don't worry we will show him, he'll regret ever messing with us," she assured me.

And just like that I'm assured.

## Chapter SIXTEEN

I'm rubbing my forehead and thinking hard about Jase. I'm back in my room and its past midnight already and at the same time I'm hoping that dad doesn't suddenly get up and come to check up on me, he'd be pissed if he knew I'm up and awake past midnight on a school night, not that school is that important anyway. But he always thinks it is, he thinks everything is.

I'm grounded and I just wish I wasn't.

I'm always getting up to this odd thing or other that he doesn't approve off.

Jules thinks it's only normal at our age. And that's when you'd think she's older than me. But she isn't but just sometimes she acts a whole lot older than her age.

It gets a little confusing for me when she does that.

I get perplexed and anxious.

A friend of yours, a dear buddy of yours goes missing one night in your bedroom or let's face it, bathroom and then your remaining closest friend starts acting a little off. She's still her old dreary self but lately it's as if she's taken Adult Pills to get her into a mature version of herself.

I crack my knuckles and lean back on my swivel chair by my desk.

I write:

**Plan of Action:**

And even underline it.

    1) Get Jase back
    2) Get Jase back safely

3) Tell Jules that you have a crush on her
4) Warning: Your life can be over, depending on how she reacts to point 3.

I start feeling all guilty again.

I'm not meant to think that my life could be over just because of Jules's reaction to the news of my crush, I'm meant to be more concerned with finding Jase in time and safe.

"I'm an evil boy."

I dread hearing the reality of who I am but I have to be honest with myself. It's others outside of me that I can lie to, just not me.

So, I jot down:

**George's Plan of Action**

Then I write:

**Jules's Plan of Action**

Then I just take the notebook and scribble a little more in it and open my desk drawer and throw it in and jam it shut.

I walk over to my bed, throw my clothes on the ground and dive into bed, sincerely hoping that I'd get some sleep for a change.

But by the next morning I realize why I never did get any sleep. It's because I'm sleeping with the enemy, at the crime scene – my bedroom with my bathroom.

## *Who would dare fall asleep there?*

### Chapter SEVENTEEN

Days swing by and my 2 plans of action remain in my notebook with barely any effort of a plan to follow – no tracks – no leads – none but that loathsome Sheriff Don. And so I give in.

"You're giving in too easily," reminds me Jules.

"No I'm not," I say, manning up.

"Yeah you are," she says stubbornly.

"How?" I ask her stupidly.

"You're letting Sheriff Don get away with it."

"What?!" I'm shocked as she has very little faith in me.

"Yeah, your letting him solve this case and Georgie we both know you were never like this in the past."

"Stop it Jules, I'm warning you, I don't like to talk about the past…"

She interrupts, "Why not? You were great as part of the Famous Five, don't you remember all the cases you solved?"

"We never solved a missing person's case Jules," I said trying to remain calm at the thought of my early years.

"Yeah but when I first met you, you wouldn't shut up about all those adventures you had with them, it was like watching a TV Series that's determined to be a part of my daily life whether I like it or not."

As an afterthought she says, "You never cared if I enjoyed hearing all about it."

"Okay," I said.

"Anything else?" I asked.

"Why are you so nonchalant about this?"

"I've told you this many times before Jules but you never ever listen. I'm not the same George of the Famous Five – you gotta believe me."

"No you are, don't be silly, I know you are," she says insisting.

"Jules, the George in the Famous Five is a girl not a boy like me!" I yell at her hoping that she listens.

"And just in case you don't believe me then I googled the Famous Five and this is what I got," he declares as he takes out a piece of paper and starts reading it to her.

- " **George (Georgina)**
  Main article: George Kirrin from http://en.wikipedia.org/wiki/The_Famous_Five
  
  *Georgina is a tomboy and insists that people call her George. With her short hair and boy's clothes she is often mistaken for a boy, which pleases her enormously. Like her father, Quentin, George has a fiery temper. She is fierce and headstrong, but very loyal to those she loves. She is sometimes extremely stubborn and*

*causes trouble for her mother as well as her cousins. She is very possessive of Timmy, her dog. George is cousin to siblings Julian, Dick and Anne and is aged eleven at the start of the series. In one interview Enid confessed that George was based on herself."*

I fold the paper and rest my case. Jules on the other hand starts talking nonsense about how I planned this and actually made up everything I just read to her just to get her off my case. Some people are really just too much. That's the first day I found out that she could be that way.

## Chapter EIGHTEEN

"Why did she always nag me about being a part of the Famous Five? And at this time?

I scream out in my bedroom, scream at the walls in anger.

Because we both know that I'd never scream at her or can get angry with her, because she's just Jules. And I think she knows it.

## Chapter NINETEEN

An hour later, my voice is coarse with all the screaming and I'm sitting on my living room coach and watching a sitcom when:

There is a knock at the door, a gentle one.

I walk over to the door and without a second thought open it.

"Hi there kiddo."

It's Sheriff Don. Just the man I needed to see.

"Hi," I say the minimum and allow him in.

"Is your dad in?" he asks looking carefully around the living room as if he may be hiding away from him behind the TV set or under the coach.

"Nope sorry."

"Do you know when he'll be back?" he asks his eyes finally settling on me.

"Nope," I say quietly.

"Okay, cheerio then," he says smiling at me. The first smile since he had entered nearly 5 minutes ago.

I smile back, cringing and biting down hard, clenching my teeth.

He leaves just as easily and quietly as he first came. I go back to watching my sitcom that is nearing its end and swear at him under my breath for making me miss some important parts of it.

## Chapter TWENTY

"…. You're saying what?"

It's Jules on the phone.

"I don't get it."

"No, no, no!" It can't be! It just can't be!!!" I yell down the receiver, drop it onto the kitchen counter and run upstairs to throw on any jeans and T-shirt and run to Jules's house to make sure that what she's told me is true, real and not a lousy joke gone bad.

Moments later, her mum swings open the door before I get a chance to ring the door bell and welcomes me in.

That's the second I see Jules crying in her uncle's embrace.

I'M SCARED – PETRIFIED EVEN.

Her eyes meet mine and I start crying like a baby boy, an uncontrollable baby boy.

I scream on the top of my lungs and both her parents suddenly turn to me.

"I hate Sheriff Don!"

But they look amazed and bewildered and I just can't understand why.

Only Timothy who I just suddenly realize is on the same page as I am and is busy comforting me by rubbing himself against my legs and keeping me warm.

My tears begin to sting my eyes, my vision gets blurry and ………..

### Chapter TWENTY-ONE

Jules and everyone else look at me and:
I remember how the world got painted all black that day – just soo black.

### Chapter TWENTY-TWO

"Why did you do that Sherrriiiifff!" I scream at the top of my lungs just outside his Police Station.

And I'm not leaving until he gives me my answers and he has to give them to me right now.

"Come out you incredibly stupid man!" I scream in harmony with my own quivering desperate voice.

"Come out Sheriff!" I scream some more.

I continue screaming that day until I turn blue in the face.

That morning the Sheriff did not get out of the Police Station, he just stared at the boy that was the town's sweetest boy turned bad in the face of a tragedy.

That's why nobody called the security on him – that's why everybody and every local town's police let him be – they just let him be.

That boy, Georgie is his name was dead exhausted and tired that night as he laid his head down to rest on his pillow in his bed that evening.

But deep inside he knew that Sheriff's latest lead, latest clue was a mislead, a wrong turn, the wrong direction, away from the path that would lead us to Jase – alive and well.

"Tomorrow we have to; we must start our own group of detectives with me as the Sheriff because that's the only way we will find Jase."

I kept repeating that until I fell asleep. I stopped counting sheep to fall asleep from that evening and started reciting that sentence until I fell asleep every night – or until the night I find Jase or Jase finds me or us – his friends and Timothy the dog.

And I solemnly swore to that and I take my oaths seriously.

### Chapter TWENTY-THREE

The next morning I read in the **Daily Newspaper**:

*"It appears to be that Sheriff Don has finally got a lead in the investigation of Jason's disappearance. His red jumper was found at what some foresee as a possible scene of the crime. Forensics confirms no finger prints and so the evidence has been discarded in this investigation until further*

*notice. This finding has bewildered the police rendering the investigation redundant. This has come at an unfortunate time for Jason's parents Mr. and Mrs. Donnavue who have just been admitted to the local town hospital. They are now in the Cardiac Department with little to no visiting hours. Their hours will be extended within a couple of days to allow relatives to visit. The local town's ……………………………………………… ……………………………………………… ……..."*

I couldn't bring myself to read the rest.

Sheriff Don has messed up so much that he had affected the health of Jase's parents. Someone had to stop him and that person is going to be me.

"Jules come on let's go to school."

"Why are we going to school on a weekend?" she asked looking at me.

I wish she would always look at me that way, full of wonder and concern.

"Did you read the Daily Paper?"

"Yes I did," she said quietly looking away.

"Well you probably don't know this but do you know that the night he disappeared he never wore a red jumper?"

He had on a T-shirt that said, "Guns 'n' Roses Are Smoking Hot" with a mariwana leaf above that tag line.

"What are you saying Georgie?"

"I'm saying that if Don keeps at this he will destroy any real chance of finding Jase."

She gets up and walks over to me plants a little kiss on my left cheek, turning it bright red and leaves.

I follow her.

### Chapter TWENTY-FOUR

We get to school and climb in through the fence.

As we enter the once jam packed Common Room we wince for being here in the weekend, it almost feels like we are being punished.

I make calls on my cell to my friends and tell them to meet us for a top secret meeting in an hour in the Common Room on the school grounds. I find it rather difficult to convince many of them that we are not in detention and just trying to get some company or worse yet trying to get them in detention too.

Kids find it difficult these days to imagine not being in detention yet wanting to hang out in the school on a weekend – a bright Saturday morning, the brightest of mornings.

But kids know me here – anything's possible with me – I guess that's why they like me – I'm not as boring as most people in this mundane Upstate New York town.

## Chapter TWENTY-FIVE

"Hey man what's up?" says Derek as he walks in and joins us.

"Wait until we all get here and …"

"We will tell you then," Jules finishes off my sentence.

"Okay but this better be good," says Derek making himself comfortable as he sits on the corner of a desk in the centre of the room.

"Hey morning guys," says Lucy as she walks in and greets us.

We all nod in her direction and Jules gets up and walks over and hugs her.

"Girls," says Derek looking at me as if I held the code to understanding them.

"You know Jules," he says as if he's explaining our connection but failing at being understood.

"Okay we are waiting for…."

"No you're not, I'm here," says Nancy as she walks in and interrupts my almost speech. She stands right in front of me waiting to hear what this is all about.

"Okay guys I brought you all here…."

"We brought you all here…" corrects Jules immediately wasting no time on anything.

"We brought you all here," I say making her comfortable which has always been important to me, "because Jason has been missing for over a month now and Sheriff Don is useless so far…"

Before I could continue, Nancy jumps in and says, "I'm pretty sure we've all seen the Daily newspaper today about that red jumper that never existed and the no finger prints crap."

"Never existed? I ask puzzled.

"Yeah that's what I gathered after reading the article, I mean who cannot get hold of any finger prints on a jumper?" she explains as all eyes face her one by one.

We all gather around her and decide there and then that we will take matters into our own hands.

"The police are not being effective and with each day we are growing that much farther away from the truth of what really happened to Jason on that night."

Everybody agreed with Jules, this much was certain.

"So what do we do, or what do you guys suggest we do?" asks Derek.

"It's simple," I say and gather us all in together.

"Let's put all our heads together and get to the bottom of this because we all know if Jase is here now, he would have done the same for every one of us."

Our meeting came to a close and after what seemed like forever, I finally started smiling again. It's a good start and I think we all felt it.

I had found my courage and the rest will all fall into place with just a little or a lot of hard work.

It was the first Saturday in a month that was great.

That's when I found out the point of reading any newspaper, it's when you can go ahead and do something to help out otherwise why bother reading something and doing nothing about it afterwards?

## **Chapter TWENTY-SIX**

The next few days were spent lurking around my house trying to gather some clues and reciting the event of that evening in excruciating detail and of course noting it down. At first we had to gather all our facts before we draw on the leads and clues and the overall direction of our personal investigation.

## Chapter TWENTY-SEVEN

## MONTH 2

"THIS sucks!" screamed Lucas.

"We have been meeting up every single day and we are no nearer to finding him – we know NOTHING."

His voice resonated in the hollow sphere above us in the design of the ceiling.

"Man relax things will take a turn for the better," said George.

"I'm sure that they will but I just can't see it at the moment…" his voice trailed off.

Jules jumped up on the table and started dancing the hokey pokey dance, twirling her waist back and forth and giggling in the process.

Lucas laughed at her. "You look hot and strange," he smiled as he walked over to the table and watched her sway to the rhythm of the music.

George went up to Jules and smiled, "You're really something," he said out loud trying to get her attention as she continued in the dancing limbo move.

Before long the whole gang: Derek, Lucas, Lucy, Nancy, Jules and I were busy doing the hoola hoola on the school grounds and the I pod was turned up to the max as it jolted song after song.

A couple of hours later, the music had slowed down to a stop and Jules was by my side, her head on the desk in front of her as she took a little nap.

"Jules, maybe we should talk," I said quietly.
She looked up at me from the desk and mouthed the words: 'not now.'

Jules was always dependable like that.

"Okay Jules whatever you say," I said as I got up and went to the toilet.

As I opened the toilet door, I saw Jules leaning on the sink in the men's toilet.
"Jules what are you doing in here?"

"I'm waiting for you, besides Lucas is starting to give me a headache."

"Why? What's he doing to you?" I ask smiling, trying to tease Jules a little.
"Stop it Georgie, I'm being serious after you left to the toilet, he wouldn't let me sleep, he had to come over and sit next to me and start nagging about Jase."

She paused looking at me, I nodded for her to continue.

"What about Jase?"

"Well how we haven't found anything yet about his disappearance."

"I know it's been tough on all of us for the same reason."

"Come on Jules let's go back there, the rest of the gang is waiting for us."

I lead the way out of the toilet and back to the Common Room.

As soon as I enter the Common Room, Lucas runs to me and says, "Listen Georgie we really need to start discovering some clues about Jase's disappearance, it's getting depressing that we don't know anything yet."

I glance at Jules and she just grabs her rucksack and exits the room.

"Lucas you really need to calm down, we are all upset that we still have no leads but we are doing all we can," I say trying to convince him as much as myself.

"By the way Lucas, where is the rest of the gang?" I ask as I scan the now empty Common Room that was filled with laughter and dancing only half an hour back.

"They all left Georgie."

"Georgie," said Lucas patting my shoulder, "I know that you are doing your best but you have to admit that our best is not good enough – if we don't start doing something productive then we may as well leave it up to Sherriff Don."

I wince hearing his name, his name just made my skin crawl.

"We will do something and something big, I promise you."

"Soon?" he asked almost in a sarcastic tone.

"Just wait and see," I say reassuringly.
"Wait and see?" he asks looking puzzled.

"Yeah, wait and see," I repeat sounding like a broken record.

I solemnly swore that day that I would make a difference in Jason's investigation, it didn't matter what kind of difference or how big or small of an impact it would make but it just had to be worth a difference in this investigation. And the worst part of it all? I had no clue, no damn clue about where to begin or how – absolutely no idea.

I just knew I had to force it out of myself.

That's how I got the smart idea of searching Sheriff Don's office in the middle of the night but of course stealing the keys to the local sheriff's police station and his office too.

The next day I sat in front of Jules and told her my idea. She laughed at me.

"What? Are you crazy?" she asked in mid laughter.

"What's so funny?" I asked my pride and ego a little bruised from her reaction.

"You want to commit a felony to help find Jase?"

Her face was filled with wonder.

"You're looking at it the wrong way, if I try to find some clues in his office, it may help us find Jase or at least give us an idea of how to find him, we need to start somewhere," I pleaded with her to see my point of view and to agree with me.

"And what if we don't and what worse, if we actually get caught?"

Her face went cloudy with the possibility looming over her head.

"Don't be negative like that, you need to be a little positive here – we are working with very tough odds."

"Please Jules strap on a pair."
As soon as I said it I regretted it.

"I'm sorry Jules I didn't mean that – it just came out wrong," I said begging her to understand.

But she didn't, she just stormed out leaving me alone with my thoughts and Felony Plan.

The next day I found Jules in the Ice Cream Parlor.

"Hey Jules," I said and waved at her from the growing queue at the cashier counter. She turned her head away from me as a response.

My heart tightened as she did that.

"Jules," I said as I walked by her table and just stood there waiting for her to let me sit down next to her.

"Go away George," she said with a quick wave of her hand.

"Jules I said I'm sorry so what more do you want me to say?" I asked really confused by her over reaction which is so typical of Jules in any situation.

"Look George I'm not upset but I do think that things are beginning to get out of hand."

"I don't get you," I said meekly.

"Sit down George," she said finally charitably offering up a smile.

"You actually want to commit a felany by sneaking into Sheriff Don's office. Isn't that going a little too far? Well, say something George."

"I told you that I'm not looking to make things worse here, Jules you know that," he said as he looked at her with all the sincerity masqueraded in his eyes.

"Worse, George? Things are already really bad."

"Yeah and they will get much worse if you don't watch out and if we both sit still and do nothing about it."

"Okay if it's such a great idea then how come you haven't told the rest of the gang about it?" she asked challenging me.

"Okay then I will make a deal with you. Starting tomorrow I will tell all the gang about the plan and then will you go ahead with it Jules, seriously?"

"Yes I will but why did I have to corner you like that to get you to tell the rest of our friends?"

"Jules I can tell them the grander scheme of things but just not things like this."

I walked over to her and held her by the shoulders, looking into her eyes I said, "Things like this need to stay private between me and you, our secret only."

She walked away from me and said, "If that's the way you truly feel.."

"I do," I said reassuringly.

"Then why did you even create this gang in the first place especially if you don't trust them enough to include them in all our plans that we are making to help us find Jase?"

"I don't know," I said feeling rather embarrassed and looking down at my shoes as I played with a little pebble on the street just outside the Ice Cream Parlor.

"Well Georgie its time you know," she said just before she turned around, walked away leaving me all alone with my thoughts.

I spent the rest of the afternoon walking in and out of my local suburban town and just thinking a thousand miles a minute.

"One thing came out of this conversation Jules, after all my walking and sulking around this town," I told her the next day.

"Sulking?" she asked.

"Yeah sulking because things are getting pretty stressful for me these days but that's not the point – the point is that you are right, right about the fact that I don't trust the same friends that I gathered into our gang."

"So?" she asked waiting for my punch-line, my conclusion, the last chapter in a book.

"So I will get them all in on the plan and see how and what they think we should do Jules, so how's that for you now? Any better?"

"Much better Georgie," she said as she pinched my right cheek and cuddled me.

"So, when shall we tell them?"

"We?" she asked looking a little bit surprised.

"Yeah, me and you will tell them."

"What Georgie? I thought you were going to tell them a—"

"Alone?" I finished off her sentence, my eyebrow raised in a quizzical question mark.

I laughed and grabbed her tickling her, "You're not going to get away that easily from all the drama Jules but I've got to hand it to you, nice try, yup nice try," I laughed some more as her laughter became a little higher than my own.

### **George & Jules Tell The Gang The Plan**

"So can somebody please just tell us all why we are back here again?" said Lucas growing impatient with George and Jules that called in another meeting in the same week.

"Yeah, what's the deal guys? Meeting twice in the same week when we only usually meet on Saturday mornings?" Nancy asked smiling mischievously.

"Well…" said George looking at Jules. "Would you like to take over here Jules," he asked half snorting into a grunted laugh.

"Okay guys, there is something we've been thinking of doing – another plan that could help us maybe find Jase or maybe just find a clue that can finally kick off the direction of this case."

As I looked at all my friends one by one, Lucas, Nancy, Lucy and Derek I noticed how all of them were pulled like a magnet to Jules's words. That's exactly the minute I realized that I wasn't the only one that's attracted to her like a magnet. Although the attraction may be a little different – the way I feel about her comparing how my friends all feel about her but the reality is that we are ALL attracted to her like a magnet- simply in one way or the other.

"Okay but how do we search for clues if we have no idea where to start looking?" asked Derek looking puzzled with the whole idea.

"Great question Derek, I know," I said pointing at my chest, "where we can start searching," I said as one of the biggest smiles settled over my whole face.

"Yeah he does," said Jules seconding what I'm saying.

"Well what is it then?" asks Lucy her eyes wide with mystery and intrigue.

"Jules and I will sneak into the Local Sheriff Police Station and sneak into Sheriff Don's office and start digging around in his office and look into his files," I announced in an authoritative voice.

"Isn't that breaking in, Georgie?" asks Lucy as she nails the problem right in the groin.

"Yeah it will be called that only.." I answer.

"Only if we get caught," emphasizes Jules again finishing off my sentence.

"Maybe that's too much of a high risk guys, you can get caught and have a record," says Lucas.

"True," says Nancy, "But then again where there's a will, there's a way Lucas," she nods her head in agreement, "I really think if is this is carefully planned it could actually work!" she says as she jumps up on the desk and towering above us all, says, "We gotta do something! All those in favor of the plan raise your hands now!"

Three hands soar above – Derek, Lucy and Nancy's.

Of course Jules and I are not part of this consensus.

"All those not in favor of the plan, raise your hands now!" she chirped as she remained towering above us.

Lucas's hand shot up in a second.

As she jumped off the table, she said, "Sorry there Lucas, out of all the 4 of us, 3 of us think that this plan is awesome!"

"So it's been decided then," I say as I smile cheekily in the direction of Jules.

"Shut-up Georgie," says Jules laughing at the same time. "It was my idea to tell them."

"But yeah because you weren't on board with this plan and wanted to see what our friends thought," I say smiling at her, teasing her.

"You wouldn't know a good plan if it bit you in the ass," I laughed throwing at her my note pad.

"Just shut it Georgie," she demanded throwing at me her pen that landed in my lap.

"Ooohh, so threatening Jules," I laugh as I pick up her pen and start writing down the notes of the plan.

## That Night In My Bedroom

That night in my bedroom, I find myself so relieved that we're finally going to do something that we've decided to move in one way, act and then see what happens.

God how much I hate that Sheriff – he's really something, that bastard!

As that thought roamed around in my head I quickly started to look for the paper that Sheriff Don first gave to my dad just after the disappearance of another kid in this town. A kid that until this day remains missing, his family has fallen apart and his mum committed suicide nearly 2 years after the day her son first disappeared.

"Jules just listen to me…"
I am pleading for Jules to hear me out on the phone.

"What is it Georgie? Are you going to bad mouth the sheriff again, you don't think that I'm tired of hearing all about it?"

She exhaled, fed up with my constant nagging about the Sheriff, all of which she's sure she's heard before and from me none the less.

"Jules, I want you to know that there's more that I have against the Sheriff other than his mistake with the red jumper that he found in a ditch in the woods.."

"Stop it George!" Jules screamed into my ear.

"Remember Jerry?" I asked pausing for effect.

A minute later, "Who's Jerry, George?" she asked sounding still peeved off with me.

"Jerry the boy that went missing nearly 4 years ago, Jerry Mac'pheet, the kid that's still missing, remember his case Jules?" I asked holding my breath begging her to remember.

"Oh gosh, yes I remember him, the one that his mum committed suicide?"

"Yes (I paused) him."

A silence crept up on us that lasted almost two full whole minutes.

"What about him?" she asked unsure whether she wanted to hear what I had to say.

"Sheriff Don gave a paper to dad about Jerry a couple of years ago and I remember reading it and making a copy of it, but I don't remember why."

"Okay and?" asked Jules unsure how to connect the dots together.

"And I must have done that because something in the letter sounded a little strange or mysterious otherwise I'd have no reason to make a copy of it and Jerry wasn't my friend, I mean we were more like acquaintances in the same school."

"So are you…..?"

"Yes, I'm looking for that photocopy in my drawers; I know I hid it somewhere in this room."

"George, do you think that Sheriff Don is a little creepy?"

"A lot more than just a little creepy Jules, I think there's a lot more to him than first meets the eyes."

"One sec," I said as I put down the phone on my desk and opened the last drawer and gently took the drawer out of the desk, leaving a gaping hole beneath the drawer's surface were a muffled number of papers were kept and a few envelopes.

I opened the top envelope, took the paper and read it out loud:

<u>CASE Ref:</u> 45629981
<u>Missing Boy</u>
<u>Name:</u> **Jerry Mac'pheet**

*Jerry Mac'pheet went missing on January 25$^{th}$ 2009 at approximately 130 am. He disappeared from his house on Newbury*

Lane on the outskirts of Newbury Hill. He has no siblings and both of his parents discovered him missing in the early hours of the next day. They reported him immediately to Sheriff Don who refused to open a missing person's file until he's been missing for at least 24 hrs as per the policy of police standards of Newbury County.

A month after his disappearance Sheriff Don found a number of leads that came to a dead end. Unfortunately and due to the sensitive nature of this case, after Jennifer Mac'pheet committed suicide on January 25th 2011, his father Mr. David Mac'pheet demanded of the General Chief of Police of Newbury, Mr.-------------- of Newbury County to close the case.

Since then, the case has remained closed and will until further notice.

"Hey Jules, you there?" I spoke to the phone handset and heard the dial tone.

### Jerry's Description:

He's (or was) a short thin kid with blonde curls all over his head, white skin tone and dark brown eyes. His cute cheeks that he hasn't lost even as a pre-adolescent give *him a constant baby face which a lot of people fall for.*

## The Bell Rings

I rush downstairs as the bell rings and open the door.

"Hey Jules…" I say as she pushes by me into my house.

"Where's that paper Georgie?" she asks in a hurry to see it.

"Did you hear it all?" I ask.

"The first part and then decided to come over and read it myself," she said determined to see it.

"Okay come on up," I say as I lead her up the stairs and into my room.

Lying on my bed is the piece of paper; I walk over and grab it, handing it to her.

She walks back and forth in my room as she reads it out loud for both me and her.

After she's done, she just stares at me – long and hard.

"You knew all along, didn't you?" she says slowly as she starts piecing everything together.

"You knew all along, that's why you insisted on sneaking into Sheriff Don's office!" she said as she clicked her fingers in my face.

"No, I only remembered now after telling the gang about our plan Jules – you gotta believe me, why would I hide it from you?"

"You wouldn't, " she says quietly, "but maybe you've always hated him that's why when Jase suddenly went missing, you just hated Sheriff Don because you didn't want him to be the one that handles his case, although at the time you couldn't remember why you reacted to him in that way – so aggressive."

"So aggressive Jules? If you remember we both were just as loathsome about him because of the hell he put us and Jase's parents through when he supposedly found the red jumper in the ditch in the woods that belonged to Jase."

I sat down, my back to her, inhaled a deep breath and exhaled.

"You can choose to believe whatever you want, it won't change the truth one bit," I say to her obviously a little upset with Jules.

She sits down next to me and puts her arms around me, hugging me she says, "Don't be silly Georgie, I always believe you, I was just trying to make sense of it all, that's all, I promise," and as she turns around to face me, she says: "Scouts honor."

That night I chose to believe her and let it go; it's just as simple as that.

## The Next Morning After The Missing Paper About The Missing Boy

It's the early evening and I'm alone sitting in my dad's lounge, trying to drink and enjoy the embittered and enraged taste of his old malt vintage whisky.

Dad, of course is not at home, otherwise there'd be hell to pay for especially as I am drinking his adult very expensively chic whisky which quite frankly tastes like a bad dose of medicine or crap.

But I'm still drinking it, actually sipping it and every time I take one sip, my face gets screwed up and I feel like I'm letting in a little more poison into my body and numbing my throat.

But I'm still drinking it until I hear dad unlock the front door outside and I quickly rush to the kitchen with the whisky glass, empty out all its contents down the drain and put the glass in the sink with some water and green fairy liquid like dad always does. Hopefully he will mistake it for his own.

Dad peers at me through the kitchen door, "Son what are you doing? Are you actually washing dishes for a change?" he snorts back a chuckle.

"Whatever, dad," I say sounding like my own teenage self again and just walk past him swiftly and up to my room before he could get a sniff of my liquor breath.

"Son not so fast," calls out my dad at the bottom of the stairs and as I turn around to face him I smile trying to trick him into thinking that all's well and as per the usual.

"Son, are you okay?" he asks looking concerned which I must note doesn't happen often enough.

"Yeah dad I am, why?" I ask.

"Well for one you're wearing a flip flop on your right foot and a pair of Nike's trainers on your left foot," he says as he walks up the stairs to me.

"What's going on son?" he asks looking deeply into my eyes.

"Son! Are you stoned?" he asks looking right into my eyes.

"No dad, I just had 2 glasses of your whisky which is nasty tasting, yuck," I say looking back into his eyes as I reason to myself that being a little tipsy is much better than being a drug addict, okay maybe not that high-level stuff but still a stoner.

"Son what's wrong? You've never misbehaved like this before? Why are you being like a baby?" he asks looking at me with all the disappointment stamped on his face.

Looking away from his glaring eyes, I start rushing up the stairs and mutter under my breath:

"You're not mum, only mum understands me."

For some reason dad doesn't follow me upstairs at all. Maybe he realizes that it's time to cut me some slack or just maybe he knows that only mum can understand me.

Minutes later I fall into my bed, face down on the warm duvet and fall fast asleep.

### Mr.Whitemore's (dad) Description:

*He's a tall and lean, thin individual with black dark hair and dark brown eyes. His face rugged and manly with a squared angled jaw line and an 'after 5pm' shave give him the 'I can deal with anything like a real man does' look. It's only until he opens his mouth that you find his conservative, righteous attitude portrayed cleverly in his words and manners of behavior.*

## The Morning After My Tipsy-Turvy Episode

I woke up with one heck of a hang-over, my head felt like a big bruise and my stomach felt like it's been gutted in a boxing fight.

I got up and slowly walked into my bathroom and I don't know how I managed it but an hour later I was ready and showered.

I clutched my head in my hands as I looked into the medical cabinet and swallowed two Tylenols.

Three hours later in the early afternoon I walked downstairs calling out dad's name but nobody responded. Just as I was about to knock on dad's lounge door, I saw him suddenly walk in through the front door, looking all smiley.

"Son, how are you feeling this afternoon?" he asked.

"I'm okay dad just.."

"A little rough round the edges," he said as his smile grew.

"Yes but it's not funny dad."

"It is when you start acting like my baby again, do I have to lock away my whisky and liquor cabinet like I used to when you were just a baby?" he asks as he walks over to me and starts pinching my cheeks and ruffling my hair.

"Dad stop it, please," I beg him to stop.

"I will stop treating you like a baby as long as you stop acting like one, deal?" he asks looking rather smug.

"Deal," I say smiling as well.
After all it could've been much worse; he could've grounded me or lectured me silly which is what he usually resorted to in the past. Perhaps because this was my first drinking incident he was shaming me into treating me like a baby, next time, if there ever will be a next time, I know will be much worse. But after the terrible hang-over I've had this morning I vowed, took an oath not to drink anymore.

Besides I needed a clear head. I had a lot on my mind like who was the Chief of Police at the time of Jerry's disappearance and why did his name remain unmentioned in the reported official case file?

But most of all why is it that boys go missing in the same part of town during the night? At around the same time as Jase disappeared?

I squeezed my temples on the side of my head trying desperately to remember the time that Jase went to the bathroom and woke me up, the time he disappeared. But for some reason I just couldn't get my head round it.

And why is it that they both disappeared in the vicinity of their homes, or friends home?

I don't know but finding that piece of paper, remembering the past seemed to get me all the more confused. There seemed to be far too many questions without any answers.

I pulled out that piece of paper again and slowly read it and as I read the last line I remembered:

I remembered my clock next to my bed on my bedside table lighting up – the time always glows in the dark – a florescent green, and when Jase woke me up that night, lightning up my face first then his, I remember looking at the clock beside me just as he went to my bathroom.

"Oh my god, it was 130 am, "I muttered under my breath and took out my notepad and jotted down some bullet points:

Missing Boy – Jerry Mac'pheet
Missing Boy – Jason Donnahue

Both disappear at night in the same local town of Newbury at the same time: 130 am.

Both disappear in a house – Jerry's own parent's house & Jason's friend's house – my own house.

Date of disappearance?

I stopped writing and just thought long and hard. An hour later I walked down the road across the local town, by the lake and over the bridge to the local Police Station.

Clutching my piece of paper in hand and folding it into my pocket, I entered the police station.

"Hi, Sir, can I please ask you a question about a current case of a missing boy called Jason Donnahue?" I asked like I didn't even know him at all.

"And you are?" he asked as he looked up from his computer and watched me for a few seconds.

"I'm – my name is George Whitemore and…"

"I know you kid, not you personally but your father so how can I help you and be honest with me now, what interests you about this case?" he asked smiling at me once he found out that I'm Mr. Whitemore's son.

"Well he's my closest buddy – Jase, I mean Jason," I say and look away from his penetrating gaze.

"I'm sorry kid about what's happened," he says quietly and then signals for me to come closer to him and whispers in my ear, "I thought being so close and all you'd know the day he's gone missing."

"Sir I'm not talking about Jase, I'm talking about Jerry."

"Oh okay, but I thought you were asking about Jason? he asked as he watched me very closely.

"Sorry sir, I meant Jerry," I said apologetically.

"Okay then, well he went missing according to his file on the night of the 25th of January

2009, but it was filed as a missing person's report 24hrs later because…"

The police man looked up and the boy was no longer standing there, he just saw the door of the police station close with a bang.

Before he knew it I ran out of the station and started running all the way to Jules house. My legs were running with such speed that I felt like I was gliding through thin air and I just couldn't stop. I just couldn't stop as my legs raced to her house and head raced with a hundred different scenarios of Jase's disappearance.

I reached her door, huffing and puffing; I rang her bell and tried to catch my breath.

"Jules, I-I-I just found out something," I said as soon as she opened the door and I saw her face.

I huffed and puffed some more.

"Hi Georgie, you okay? Come in," she led me into her home.

"Georgie, what's gotten into you?" she asked as she watched my panic-stricken expression on my face. She rarely saw that expression.

I reached into my navy blue anorak's pocket and took out the folded somewhat crumpled piece of paper and gave it to her.

Looking at it, she reminded me, "Georgie you already showed me this, Georgie?"

"Read it out loud again Jules to me and you…"

"But," said Jules very bewildered.

"God Damn it, read it AGAIN!" I yelled at Jules, the stress getting to me.

As she read it I took out my notepad and wrote down:

Jerry first went missing on January 25$^{th}$ 2009
Jason first went missing on January 25$^{th}$ 2013

She finished reading and walked up to me and hugged me.

"Georgie, what's going on, please tell me more than this piece of paper? You look panicked."

"Jules here you go, read this in my notepad," I said as I handed her my notes on Jerry and Jason's case.

"Can't you see why I'm panicking?" I asked quietly as she read it.

Her pupils grew larger and her surprise enveloped her whole face, "Oh my god Georgie, they've both gone missing on the same day but four years apart, in the same town, even at roughly the same time," she looked at me as her eyes filled with tears.

"Jules, don't cry, but isn't this weird – it's far too many coincidences, don't you think?" I say to her in a whimper looking away.

"And that's not all Jules, I just came from the police station and that's where I found out the day that Jerry went missing but the thing is that, one of the police men in the station that was in the reception, when I told him my full name his tone changed and he became friendly because he knows dad – it seems quite well…."

"So, you know he knows Sheriff Don quite well Georgie and it is quite a small town," she explained.

"I don't know Jules, I mean you're right but I just felt that there's something a little off with my encounter with him, I don't know – call it intuition," I said feeling a lot more relaxed because I got it all out to Jules.

"I don't know Georgie but it's beginning to sound a little scary," she said as she glanced away from my gaze.

"I know I guess I just didn't expect to find out something like this, it's a little disturbing," I said as my voice trailed off.

"It's scary is what it is," she said.

"Well it's too late to stop right now, but.."

She interrupted me, "Just make sure that you don't tell anybody, incase we're onto something we don't want the wrong people to find out," she said looking at me with her soulful deep colored eyes.

"Like who Jules?" I asked not sure I understand what she means.

"I don't know, but that's the point we don't know – we can't be sure where and who those wrong people are, they could be…"

"The police," I answered.

"Exactly and you know how far reaching they are and if that's really the case then the whole police force is corrupt or one bad egg among them or the Chief of Police that has his name unmentioned at the time of Jerry's missing case."
"God, this could get very dirty Jules," I say almost sure that it's already there.

"Just our luck," says Jules.

"Jules," I say looking away from her, "it could be much worse, it could have been one of us that's gone missing instead of Jason," I say.

"Especially me, it was in my bedroom, my bathroom after all," I say almost shivering at the thought of it.

"Stop it Georgie that's only going to freak us out," she warns me.

"I don't know about you but I'm already freaked out," I answer.

"Well maybe we can help solve Jase's case and Jerry's case too at the same time," she says.

"Yeah it looks like it because they seem to be both so intertwined with one another – they are …"

"Linked," she finishes off my sentence for me.

I nod in response.

"Jules can you come and stay over at my place tonight?" I asked suddenly out of the blue.

"Like when we were little kids," I added to make it sound more natural and not like me hitting on her although God knows how much I was dying to hit on her but I dare not.

"Sure," she smiled and at once I'm relieved because it doesn't seem like she has any idea what's running through my mind about how I feel about her lately.

I smiled and winked at her.

She ruffled my hair, "What's that for silly?" she asks me teasing me playfully.

"Just trying on my charm for other girls on you," I laugh at her.

"Well don't do that cheeky wink," she says.

"Cheeky wink? I thought I'm being sexy and charming that way," I say.

She falls over the chair laughing uncontrollably.

"Georgie, you're just too funny," she says as she laughs more.

"Hey Jules cut it out," I say warning her that I may tickle her again.

"I dare you," she challenges me.

But I know better than to fall into her trap, having known her since we were in diapers.

## That Night With Jules In My Bed

We chatted for hours while we were both cuddled up in the warmth and coziness of the duvet. For a change we made a pact to take a break from all this drama and to go back where we left of just before Jase disappeared.

And somehow it had worked.

She laughed so much that night by my side and I beside hers. It made me wonder though what would happen if the laughter ever stopped? I know you might say that we've known each other since we were introduced in diapers but I don't know now a days with all that agonizing stress and confusion lurking like a cloud over our heads, if we're not laughing, we are worrying or worse we are just nonchalant about life and all that it offers.

But the good thing about tonight is that I laughed like I hadn't for what seems to be like forever. I really enjoyed her company and just wish she could stay over every day. At least in this phase of our lives but I knew that Martha, her mother wouldn't allow her to stay at my place so often.

But never mind that, as I look at her asleep next to me I smile. She really does sleep like an angel; granted she makes a whole lot of noise snoring away but still an angel.

## THE next day

It wasn't until I woke up the next day that I noticed how energetic I became after a proper full night's sleep.

"Hi dad," I called out to him out in the garden at the back.

"Hi son, how are you doing today?" he answered just behind the garden shed.

I walked around back and found him on his knees, with his brown leather gloves planting a flower in the pot with sand. He looked up and seemed distant. Dad always appeared quite distant when gardening especially in and around his shed. He is always so focused that way.

"Dad?" I tried to catch his unattainable attention.

He didn't even look up. "Dad?"

"Dad?"

"Yes, son, what is it?"

"Nothing I just wanted to say morning."

"Oh," he looked up quite surprised.

"Morning son," he said and as soon as the last syllable is out of his mouth, he gets back to business, his head down and continues planting flowers, all kinds of them.

I tear out a weed from the corner of the garden shed, grasping it in my hand I walk across the rest of the garden and back into the house.

"Oh that's a nice surprise," I say as I see the back of Jules as I walk into the kitchen to the coffee machine.

"What you doing here?" I ask with the biggest smile playing over all my features one by one.

"I could leave if you like," she teases me with an even larger smile.

"Not a chance," I grin and offer her a cup of coffee.

"Stay and you get either a cappuccino or a Mochaccino," I say as I hold up a mug of each.

"Hhhmm, I'd say a Cappuccino but by the way when did you start drinking the 'yucky' stuff?"

"Well just the other day, you know after we had that chat about that report that I found about Jerry's disappearance – that piece of paper?"

She nodded.

"Well I really felt the urge to try something completely new, so I made a cap and a moc and just prefer the taste of cap," I explain as I clean the filter of the coffee machine in the sink.

"Funny, you're an expert with the coffee machine now after only.."

"Only 3 days," I finish off her sentence.

"It's my latest craze," I look at her and take a sip of my cap.

"Well okay here goes then," she giggles and takes a sip as well.

"Well I don't know about you but I still taste the yuckiness of it," she turns her mouth into a knot and screws up her otherwise stunningly delicate feminine features.

Looking at her it just amazes me how beautiful she is – this must be an example of classical beauty and just like that I thought of her nickname, 'Black Beauty.'

"You're nickname is Black Beauty from now on," I said as I start speaking my mind.

"What?" she asks.

"You mean a horse, Disney's production of a black horse?" she asks knowing very well that I am calling her beautiful.

"You know Georgie, I just love the way you call me beautiful, you're just not direct about it," she said as she giggled a little bit.

I blushed.
With my head down I said, "Well I just love beating around the bush, it gets too damn boring to be direct all the time," I keep my head down a little longer pretending that I have to tie my undone shoe laces.

"Anyway Georgie I've got to go into town to do some boring errands like help Mum with her grocery list and drop of some mail at the local post office and stuff, wanna join?"

"Yeah why not," I say pretty pleased that the flirting has stopped. I find it rather uncomfortable to flirt with Jules who's been like my sister and best friend since like forever but I just couldn't help it today.

"Give me 5 minutes, I just need to grab my wallet and a couple of things and I will be down again," I said.

"Sure Georgie take your time, I'm not in a hurry to go grocery shopping trust me," she said as she laughed about it.

A few minutes later and we are nearing the grocery store.

"Georgie have you thought a lot about that piece of paper, you know all the similarities between the two missing boys?"

I look at her and frown, "Yeah all the time, I just can't seem to get it out of my head, no matter how much I busy myself."

"It's really doing my head in," I say and look away from her.

"Yeah sorry that I brought it up again but I just can't seem to stop thinking about it as well, it's just too much, too much of a coincidence."

"Hhhmmm, I don't know what to say Jules."

"Maybe, now just listen to this idea, just for a second okay, maybe just maybe we should search

Sheriff Don's office at the police station as you suggested but after that search you dad's home office too," she said slowly.

"What? Why would we search my dad's?" I ask unsure of whether I've just been insulted.

"Because you found that piece of paper that report in your dad's office at the beginning didn't you?" she points out.

"No Jules, that's not how it happened, I found it hidden and forgotten in my room because I'm just so messy that way," I clarify.

"Oh, I'm sorry Georgie but why would you have it already with you, I mean who gave it to you in the first place?"

"Nobody did Jules, I just saw it pinned on the Missing Boys Board at the Police Station at the time when dad was there visiting a Sheriff and just the story struck a chord of sadness with me especially as I've known Jerry as an acquaintance at school at the time, that's how it caught my attention and so without saying much I just unpinned it and took it. Nobody knew that it had been stolen off the board," I explained in full all the while watching her face change with the knowledge that she had just assumed things.

"Anyway later I discovered the Sheriff Don had given a copy to dad to keep with him in his lounge," I added.

"I'm sorry Georgie, I didn't mean to suggest anything about your dad but I thought that if you found it in his home office at first, then…. never mind….that's all," she said ashamed.

"Jules dad doesn't have a home office, he has a lounge that's like his office but different."

I shrugged my shoulders at Jules, "Don't worry I'm not upset but you're right if we don't do something and do something fast, it will drive us up the bloody wall."

She stops walking and turns on me, "So where do we start?"

"At the beginning."

We walk into the grocery store and at once I'm relived that Jules had something else to concentrate on.

### THE THE next day

"Okay Jules so let's begin by searching the Police Station after it closes tonight," I say as if what I'm saying is truly the easiest thing to do in the world.

"Say it like it is Georgie," she says.

"It's breaking an entry tonight so let's just say it like it is," she says determined to phrase things just perfectly.

"You know Jules I don't know if you're aware of it yet or not but this mission is not going to succeed if you just phrase it properly," I say sarcastically.

"Whatever Georgie, so what's the plan then for tonight for Tom Cruise?" she asks taking the sarcasm a notch further.

"Well I think we need to get hold of the night cleaner's uniforms and then we should be sorted, its easy sailing from there," I say thinking out loud.

"How do you figure that?" she asks.

"Well I've noticed a cleaner's schedule in the bathroom of the men toilets there, on more than one occasion and I realized that it includes the shifts at night, they include the name and time of signing in for duty and signing out. I can easily get hold of that schedule and then all we have to do is get our hands on two uniforms," I say with a click of my finger.

"And where do we get that?" she asks.

"That part I'm still trying to work on but it's our best bet because once we get the names and uniforms then we will just buy the wigs that are needed," I pause and think it all through.

Jules stares at me.

"You seem to have already given this a lot of thought Georgie."

"Yeah remember it was originally my idea that's why so I've had a lot of time to think about how to do it," I remind her.

"Well you're doing a good job from the sounds of it," she says.

"Finally Jules I get a compliment from you," I say.

"No really Georgie, it's good to know that you're on top of things because most of the time I feel like I'm just about to lose it," she admits meekly.

"Don't worry Jules, your safe and I promise you that, we are both safe and that's definitely a promise," I say trying hard to comfort her obvious over anxious mind.

"So after we get the uniforms and names sorted out, what's next?"

"The hardest thing about all this is that we need to figure out the exact time we should be on the premises, the time that the so called cleaners are on duty and that's when we need to figure out a way to have them on duty that same day, the same instant we are searching Sheriff Don's office."

I pause and look away deep in thought.

"But that's where another problem arises, if we are at the same time on duty, then we have to make sure that the cameras don't catch two cleaners of the same name on the premises at once otherwise we're busted."

"I don't know Georgie but the more you explain it the more complicated it gets," she says a little worried that Georgie is just getting too carried away by all the movies he watches.

"No there's a way around the cameras but the thing is that it's going to take a pretty long time to figure it out," he says still deep in thought as his eyes sparkle.

"I can get my hands on the Police Station's blue print – the latest one – and from there we can figure out the camera points and angles, so after we study them closely we can memorize their locations and work our way around them so that the only cleaners that are ever on record are the genuine cleaners and not us."

I smile a large and satisfied smile and look at Jules.

"Wow you think you can pull it off Georgie?" She asks really starting to get impressed with his ways.

"Well Jules here's the thing – I kinda have to," I say confidently.

"But Jules I need your help on this, we really need to cover all our grounds before going in just to make sure that we are never caught or if anything goes wrong we can lie our way out of it without any evidence to prove otherwise," I say carefully.

"So if we get caught by one of the police men or one of the security guards or even cleaners, even if they see us we still need to make sure that it's their word against ours and that's all."

"That sounds like a hell of a lot Georgie," says Jules looking concerned.

"No Jules it's the contrary because if they just see us but they can't prove that they did in the confines of a secure camera system and finger prints at the Police Station then they have nothing."

I look at her – watch her expression as it changes from concern into a cheeky grin.

"Maybe we're ready then Georgie," she says and laughs.

"You find this funny?" I ask surprised.

"No I just think that if we pull it off without a hitch then we've proven a lot," she says.

"Like what?" I ask wanting to desperately hear her approval of our first mission together.

"We are a good team," she says.

"Jules finally – it only took you a good 1 hr to get to this conclusion, you truly are a handful," I say teasing her.

"Well I can't give in to you so easily, can I?" she says as she starts teasing me too.

"Why not?" I ask feigning ignorance.

Of course it's a question that she chooses to ignore.

## **THE THE THE next day**

Lucas looks out of his window and yawns at the trees just lurking behind his white picket fence. It's

3pm already in the afternoon but he is still yawning and wearing his most comfortable light blue pj's. These are his personal favorites for a reason that nobody would understand. There is a lot about Lucas that people don't understand.

On one hand he's as easy to talk to as a diary and on the other as rigid as they come. His mentality is just a little bit on the harsh side. And people seldom admire him for it.

He's known to be the level headed boy of the gang, the one that keeps them at bay, safe from riding out into the storm or experimenting with substances that can leave their impact and imprint on life. He's both as interesting and as boring as they come.

Interesting because he's full of contradictions that work and boring because he's as predictable as they come. People have often mocked him for his predictability saying he's as sure as desert weather. As we all know there is only one constant climate in a desert and that's hot.

Girls find him irresistible at first and then somehow his mentality starts to push them away. His tolerance of others is limited and his understanding of others likewise and that's how he has become the butt of all jokes in the gang but he knows better than to let it get to him.

You see that's the thing about Lucas, people can say many things about him but being stupid is definitely not one of them. He carries around with him finesse, sophistication, an intelligence that is hard to match.

Above all, the way he carries himself day in day out says it all; he's a sensible, educated boy that is limited by the restrictions that he places around him; the rules he makes up in his life that he insists on following amid a wreck of contradictions.

So the fact that Lucas is staring outside his window at 3pm and still yawning and in sleep wear, well let's just say it as it is, that's a normal day for him, a normal start to the day when schools out.

Sometimes he's just as lazy as they come and today is no exception.

He suddenly hears a knock at the front door and walks to the window that overlooks the entrance and carefully takes a little peek at whose standing at his front door.

As he looks at Virginia outside he gets an inkling of the hurt she had caused him almost a year ago and he's at once rooted to the ground, unable to budge an inch.

She knocks once more, waits around for a few seconds and just as she looks like she's about to discover his hiding place behind the curtain of that particular window, she leaves and walks away.

"She walked away," he says under his breath to no one in particular. And just as he says it, he is reminded of the moment she walked away from their love affair leaving him with his head hung low and his heart broken into pieces, leaving him to figure out how to glue the pieces back together to make him whole again.

Something that took him just about a year to do.

And now as if his heart had spoken to her and told her, summoned her to walk back into his life again – his heart must be proud of this achievement of 'putting himself back together, ' and so called upon her to come and have a look at the pieces that were once broken and now glued together stronger than ever before.

But this is Virginia we're talking about and she just never learns. As time passes by, people come in and out of her life, some linger on for a little while longer while others are short stays, but somehow Virginia being Virginia just doesn't seem to notice the speed and strength of the human race.

Virginia only notices Virginia and therein lays the problem.

So in all fairness although Lucas was called into the gang after Jase's disappearance he never felt at home with the boys and girls in his gang.

"It's nice of George to include me," he mutters under his breath at no one in particular.

But the other day when George & Jules called the gang in for an emergency meeting, he thought not much of it but when they told them why they were summoned, he got all worked up and concerned.

Desperate to find a clue or lead to start working with, Georgie decided that he should almost rob the Police Station – of course rob it off its privacy via arranging a break in to search Sheriff Don's office.

Since that Wednesday Lucas has been toying with the idea of blowing their cover before it's too late and calling Sheriff Don and telling him all about their disrespectful and illegal deal.

But something had stirred inside of him the minute he stood in front of the Police Station and watched Sheriff Don (with his window open) scolding a sobbing young girl barely the age of 10 years.

The Sheriff's manner and tone weakened Lucas's desire to help him.

And there was something in that scolding that he couldn't quite put his finger on. It wasn't about the girl and how vulnerable she appeared or scared or even that she was so young, it was something that stirred a reaction inside of him.

Something about the Sheriff that nearly petrified him.

Something in him that until this day he's trying to figure out but can't.

Why?

Because he doesn't understand his own reaction to what happened:

"Young lady you will never behave in this manner again, do I make myself clear?" his voice rang with a dominating authority as the young girl started weeping.

"You will never behave like this again Rose or else…"

"Or else what?" her voice quivered, shivering to answer him back.

He threw the vase of flowers and sent them crashing on the floor of his office in the opposite direction of the young girl.

She screamed in shock.

"You will never behave like this again Rose, do I make myself crystal clear?" he asked almost pleading with her to show her rebellious side again and handle the dire consequences.

As she looked around the office and saw the crystal shreds and pieces broken on the floor with a bunch of beautiful flowers amidst them, she quickly nodded and hung her head low.

Lucas stood staring well after the whole episode finished and just watched as the Sheriff left the young girl in the office crying as he tended to his duties as the Sheriff careless of the young girl's presence or feelings.

After that night, Lucas stayed away from the Police Station. He had seen enough that one night to last him the whole damn year and what a year it will prove to be.

## Lucas's Description:

*He's a charming fellow with dirty blonde smooth silky short cut hair and dark hazel eyes that fool everybody that set eye on him, expecting blue or green eyes especially with that overtly fair skin tone. His face is round and chubby giving him all the more of a kid look that refuses to grow up just like Peter Pan.*

## THE THE THE THE next day

Virginia can't believe that she was just standing in front of Lucas's front door just earlier.

One thing she knows about herself is her constant need to be centre of attention. And what she heard last week in school shocked her.

She has only one way of finding out the truth and that is by contacting Lucas.

The fact that he hadn't opened the door or that he wasn't there, but she knew better than that, she knew that most probably he was there but chose not to open the door and re-connect to their past.

But she needed to know if what she heard at school is at all true. Because as rumors go this definitely is the worst of them.

But she also needed him to be completely and utterly over her because she has no energy to go through the break up and the reason why she broke up with him for the millionth and one time.

Students – kids have a knack for saying some truly ugly things. But one has to wonder has to wonder how ugly can the fabrication be and after last week she stopped wondering – it was so ugly that she simply did not want to be near anything or even any gossip about this topic – that's if it was at all true.

That's why she needed to know, and unfortunately the key to unlocking that door is tucked away neatly with her ex-boyfriend Lucas.

"Did you hear?" asked one high-schooler to another.
"About what?" answered another.
"About Jase disappearing."
"You gotta be shitting me!"
"How? You sure it's not just a rumor?"
"Well you can never tell in Maritime High but who would spread such a rumor."
"True."
"And I heard that George had a hand in all this," she whispers in the ear of her friend.
"But that doesn't make sense because George and Jase are as thick as thieves."
"Yeah but Jase apparently went missing in George's house."
"That's dodgy."
"Yeah and apparently that quite one, you know the reserved, geeky but intelligent one, what's his name again?" she asks as she tries her best to remember.

"Oh, you mean uuhhhmmm Lucas!" she says out loud as she clicks her finger in response.
"He has something to do with it too," she says just as loud.
"Noo - you're kidding what with the disappearance?" says her friend as she raises her eyebrow.

The two girls that were in the gym failed to notice a pale girl behind them by the name of Virginia.

## The First Day Of The New Week

Lucas woke up at dawn as sleep was quickly becoming to him a thing of the past, thanks to his ex-girlfriend's re-appearance in his life, even though it was only standing at his front door. She still made that move that he thought about over and over and over again. Today is the first day of the school week and he felt tired and stressed and just so many things all at once, of course again thanks to Virginia.

Virginia woke up with a start as her alarm rang wholes in her head, signaling the start of the new week at school. She hated that day, the first day of the week, of every week really. And then she remembered the whole sordid thing, the rumor she heard in the gym that day and Lucas who has always been a cause of so many headaches not to mention a little heartache from time to time. She had to find a way to talk to him, just enough to know if the rumor is true or just another of Maritimes favorite past times – gossip. She forced herself out of bed and wiggled her way in sleepy-drunkenness to the bathroom to freshen up before heading to school.

Jules wakes up and feels herself smiling at everything and nothing at all. It's amazing but since her last conversation with Georgie, it's just that she suddenly finds him attractive in a Brad Pit meets Angelina Jolie on the film set type of way. And since that day, she hasn't been able to remove his presence and hold over her mind. Now she catches herself waking up to laughter and sleeping with a smile on her face. But Jase's memory still remains fresh in her mind, nothing seems capable of erasing that.

George wakes up with a little smile and a tear drop threatening to fall down the slope of his face. He's happy and sad all at once. Such a mixed up bottle of emotions that he knows is Jase's fault but he only has one wish – to be able to blame Jase when all this is over and done with and Jase is back alive and kicking. "But I don't even have an idea when that will be," he mutters to himself in the mirror as he brushes his teeth readying himself for the first day of the week – a Monday school day.

Mr. Whitemore wakes up his eyes bloodshot and itchy as hell. Once again he welcomes the new day of the week in his lounge having fallen asleep as per the usual on another file that he's currently working on. He's still stylish as his suit is still on, the purple pinstriped shirt and the black pants to match. His tie – the darkest purple shade is still on his neck smothering him with a mother's love. He rubs his eyes, one by one and starts loosening his tie before he forces himself up off the chair, out of the lounge and up the stairs and into his room where he proceeds to peel off yesterday's work clothes today.

Martha wakes up with her dog Lassie in her bed beside her. And all that she first thinks about as she opens one eyelid after the other is Lassie and how her world would be turned upside down if it wasn't for her beloved dog. Dog lovers are universal but still most people didn't understand the bond of loyalty that an owner has with her dog, that special bond that differs considerably from one owner to the other.

Sheriff Don wakes up with pride. He's proud that he's who he is and that just about sums it all up – the first day of the week for him always begins with the praising of himself. He's never been one to rely on other's praise but he never thought of the underlying reason why he refused to rely on them to begin with. He gets out of bed and catches a glimpse of himself in the mirror where he salutes himself for himself.

They all spend the day locked in their own shell that is littered with beliefs, values and faith; their faith of themselves in the larger world. Fate they assume wrongly has nothing to do with it, or if any just very little.

The stable nature of time will prove every single one of them wrong – but then again that's the beauty of time, unbeknown to every one of them.

## The Second Day Of The New Week

Jules stands outside Maritime High waiting for her other half, George. But he's no-where to be seen and although he's late on more than one occasion – he's still a little bit too late this time.

She should be concerned, "But I'm not and I don't why," she says to herself under her breath as a couple of girls hanging on the stairs hear her and start darting glances of concern at her.

To them she appears to be a little insane – a girl speaking to herself on an autumn afternoon on the steps of the local high school – not an everyday normal activity that high schoolers routinely enjoy.

But let's face it with all the drama that's going on – it's quite surprising that Jules remains this level-headed – maybe finally Lucas started rubbing off on her; the man of sense and sensibility. Worse things can be said about her right now, "Much worse," she says to herself out loud, reminding a part of herself that she is still stable.

It's not easy to remember that stuff, "Not at all," she says much louder than she originally intended.

The same couple of girls on the stairs start walking away from where she is, finding her a little odd and of course the rumors have had their day at the high school and so most people are acting all 'weirded up' around her. But she grew to love her impact on them. "It makes me feel a little powerful," she says loudly lying to herself, because she knows that she's being over consumed by a powerful feeling that's hard to keep at bay.

Jules stands outside Maritime High waiting for her other half, George. But he's no-where to be seen and althou …..

"Hey Jules sorry I got held up with Mr. Richardson and you know how he gets talking," came George's voice over her thoughts stopping them midway.

"Hi Georgie, no worries," she says hiding from him her little conversation she had with herself on the steps of high school out loud where others nearby could actually hear her.

She didn't think it's the right time to let him in on what's happening to her – how she's coping with Jase's disappearance and all that chaotic spin off events and plans. Sometimes caring for someone meant not letting them in on your suffering, for their sake not yours of course. From that day on Jules started to think of herself as a martyr and that in itself is the most powerful feeling in the world. Martyrdom what a powerful drug induced kingdom.

George sped up to meet Jules, he didn't want her to know the real reason he's running late. He didn't want her to know how he needed to go into the toilet and throw up for like the 3$^{rd}$ time that day, his insides squeezing out of his mouth and crying out for help to be noticed. He didn't want to tell her how Jase's disappearance is making him sick, literally. Today is the first day of his sickness routine that he sincerely hopes will become a quick thing of the past and not a daily or even weekly routine. That much he knew and of course not wanting her to know anything about any of it.

Virginia is back at Lucas's front door AGAIN. It's just been a couple of days since she last visited that side of his front door. She knows more than anything else that she shouldn't be prying into other people's lives especially when she had demanded to be left in the dark. But as time flies, seasons change, people give birth while others perish the earthly world and Virginia goes back on her most damning of moments when she broke up with Lucas:

"You just don't get it! I want you and your messy bloody life out of mine, leave me alone, I'm not interested in anything you have to say anymore, don't you get that?" she said to him as she turned on her heel and walked in the opposite direction, leaving him instantly all on his own with his own loud thoughts drumming into his ear drums.

And still she's back at Lucas's front door. Some would call her insane to come back and stick her nose where it doesn't belong others a genius. Of course this depends on your definition of each term. People's definitions just differed – that's just the way it is – the way of the world – hers mostly.

As Lucas got ready to leave to go and have a milk shake with one of his buddies – ("my buddy," he thought to himself is if anything a rather strange new concept), he forgot to remember the other day that Virginia stood saluting his front door and waiting for him to come out and salute her. Some would be surprised or shocked that for a split few moments he completely forgot about her re-surfacing in his life, unwanted and unattended to. So that morning as he swung the door open, his face fell and with it his heart plummeted straight to the ground just in between his feet.

"Uhhh, Virgie," he said completely caught off guard outside his house.

"Hi Lucas, how are you?" she asked trying to sound breezy and natural yet failing horrendously at it.

"How am I?" he asked looking quite dismayed at her lack of consideration yet again.

"I'm good no thanks to you that's for sure," he said as he shoved her out of his way so that he can lock the door to his house properly.

"Oh Lucas that's not what I meant," she said putting on a pout that's meant to make him melt.

"Virgie, I don't know if you noticed or not but what you mean or don't mean to say is no longer any of my business and you'd do well to stick to your own stuff," he says with a soft voice but with a mightier tone than he's ever used with Virginia.

"Lucas," she said his name like she had a right over it.

"Stop this Virgie, this is I don't know but maybe something that is a part of your new game or you're just bored or something but trust me drop it now and walk away it's better," he said as he slowly but surely threatened her.

His threat fell on deaf ears.

"Lucas I need to know if you have anything to do with Jase's disappearance – you know people are talking and I'm hearing so many things and…."

He interrupts her and says, "Sod this! You're just here because people are talking and you want to be the 'one' that knows the truth, to be the one that is the most popular girl for knowing it all before everybody else? Wow, you're actually much worse than I thought," he says snickering at her.

"Lucas you've got it wrong I …"

"Virgie I never thought I'd ever say this to you of all people but shut the fuck up!" he screamed at her with venom clearly behind his words shielding the sharpness of his full hurt from view.

Virgie is stunned.

"Go on walk away, we both know that's what you do best!" he yelled at her and then when she didn't move he just simply walked away from her.

"It's time she knows how it feels like when somebody walks away from her without a care in the world," he grunted to himself under his breath as he marched away, down the street to meet his buddy.

Minutes later, his buddy – Kev is at the café and notices Lucas marching down the street, all hot and bothered with a red, steaming face and the weight of the world on his shoulders.

Martha walks the width of her garden for like the millionth time waiting for her lover to ring the bell. She hates waiting for him every single time but as much as she hates it, she knows that nothing can ever change UNTIL only one thing does – its made official and people know of their love affair.

She feels like a kid in love all over again, because she's hiding and lurking in the shadows just to see her man. God forbid she saw him like a normal adult in normal circumstances but those were not the men that she fancied those were the ones that bored her ridiculously with their ways.

"He's nothing like that," she said out loud facing the yellow tulip in her garden.

But that's the thing with love, it chooses you.

Mr.Whitemore as usual is in a hurry to run into the arms of his sweetheart and as usual he's late which comes as no surprise to people that know him best.

But what surprises him is his inability to control their love affair.

A control freak in nature, his way of dealing with things is by controlling them and when he can't he just shrinks away from the responsibility. But with her he just can't get away, his heart demands that he remains as close as possible to this woman. Anything else appears to cause irreparable damage to his health – his mental health that is. So, he dumps the latest file into his cabinet and walks out in a huff and puff reminding himself to pick up a bouquet of flowers for Martha who he knows is doing laps in her house by now.

Sheriff Don simply didn't get much sleep last night and he knew why. He had that constant dominant feeling that they were finally onto him and he is about to pay the heavy price for his ways. Who could sleep when that's weighing down their mind at night?

Even sleeping pills of which he took the regular dosage were not enough to keep down his nauseating worry of being caught red handed, imprisoned and sentenced.

### Virginia's Description:

*She's a little chubby around the edges, big boned and cheeky with a sarcastic look in her green striking eyes, followed by a mischievous 'hard to handle' brown dark hair that insists on being thick, wavy and not at all 'prim and proper.'*

### The Third Day Of The Week

All of them – Sheriff Don, Martha, Mr.Whitemore, Jules, George, Virginia and Lucas were in frenzy that evening.

All panic stricken to deal with Jase's disappearance like their lives depended on it.

Sheriff Don was busy drinking away his nauseating worry over himself in a bar round the corner from the restaurant were Martha and Mr.Whitemore were dinning in seclusion and privacy on the side of the corner of where George and Jules were about to enter into the cinema to watch the latest blockbuster were they were going to come into a head's on collision with Virginia and Lucas arguing in the cinema foyer before the movie starts.

"You're such an ass Lucas," she says still angry that he walked away from her that day.

"Well you've been one for so long it's only fair to show you how you've acted all along," he says as she watches his words set her world aflame with more fiery outbursts.

"You're such a…"

"Hey Lucas what you doing here with Virginia?" interrupted Jules looking from one set of eyes to the other as they both stared at her in disbelief.

"Oh, Jules," says Virginia unsure of what to say and so looks away.

"George," says Lucas and also looks away uncomfortably.

"Guys if you're back together then why hide it, just tell us," smiles George at them both.
"We're not," says Lucas.

"Yeah we're not and you know why guys, it's because Lucas can't get over the past so much so that he's fucking up the present as we even speak," she said smiling at them all politely and excusing herself.

She leaves the cinema crying but nobody is aware of her tears but herself and she reminds herself that it's the only way it's meant to be.

## The Fourth Day Of The Week

Most of them slept, ate and had long conversations over the phone the whole day and night. Those that had work called in sick and those that had school called in sick as well. The only two of them that were no longer on speaking angry terms were Virginia and Lucas. Their tones had changed, their voices had calmed down a couple of notches and their anger had subsided leaving them with nothing to talk about.

## **The Last Day Of The Week**

Lucas woke up at dawn as sleep was quickly becoming to him a thing of the past, thanks to his ex-girlfriend's re-appearance in his life, even though it was only standing at his front door. She still made that move that he thought about over and over and over again.

Just as much as things change, they stay the same. That's certainly true of Lucas and Viginia – theirs was a love of the most destructive kind, they loathed to love each other and loved to loathe each other all at the same time. The result is as disastrous as can be expected, perhaps the only thing they could agree on or knew for sure is that in life you can only expect the unexpected and live by it, hand in hand.

## **The Plan Nears**

As the days gave into other days, the nights into other nights and the mornings whizzing by, the time to action the plan got nearer and nearer still.

Jules started waking up with the adrenalin lift of riding a rollercoaster and Georgie started feeling like he was truly invincible.

A combination both lethal and that induces a surplus of confidence in both friends.

"Hey Jules we're gonna crack it," said Georgie in full swing of the plan.

"Crack it? You mean we're gonna nail it," said Jules laughing.

"What's funny?" asks Georgie innocently.

As Jules blushed and Georgie enjoyed her growing reddish glow on her cheeks, she just thought she may as well just blurt it out now; "Nailing it can be.." and she started trying to hand gesture the whole thing.

A minute later of strenuous hand gestures and Georgie fell on the grass chuckling.

"You can't even say it Jules!" he laughs even harder but that's one thing he loves about Jules, her innocence.

"Back to the plan Georgie, your moment is over," she says grinning and secretly hoping to distract him so that she can return to her usual shade of light pink in her cheeks.

"Okay, okay Jules take it easy, well there's no point in rehearsing it again Jules, we know it so well – it's like we've become the leading actors on the set of the movie – Police Station Robbery –Minus The Robbery."

"It sounds like a comedy that takes the piss out of movies about Robberies," she says smiling and thinking that this idea could actually work in the entertainment industry.

"Yeah true just like that comedy that took the mock out of horror movies, "The Scary Movie," he said as he doubled over with laughter as he remembered the main villain 'Screamer' having a Budweiser beer and answering the phone screaming "What's Uuuuupppp," which is Budweiser's TV Ad slogan.

"Georgie stop laughing this is real, its not fiction," she says all serious all of a sudden.

"I know Jules, I know," he says as he walks over to her and hugs her long and hard. But he couldn't tell whether the hug was to comfort him or her. But that didn't really matter, not now, not in the scheme of things.

## The Day Before The Plan

Jules and Georgie were both lying down in his bedroom being silly and fooling around as they played Twister just to take their minds off the big following day.

## The Morning Before The Plan Takes Place

She rushes to Georgie's house and finds him sitting down on the front steps of his place, knotted in deep thought.

"You better not be thinking of calling it all off," she says sarcastically.
"No I'm not," he answers in an overtly serious tone.

She looks at him and wonders what really is at stake here. She doesn't come up with anything and so carries on like it was just another day.

## The Night Before The Plan Takes Place

They are both lying down again almost half asleep.

She turns to him and sees how his eyes appear glued to the TV screen and says, "Do you think people about to rob something are as calm as we are just hours before their mission?"

He looks at her and says, "Well maybe but then that really depends on their character."

Jules notices again how a few days before the mission takes place Georgie changed into a friend that insists on speaking to her in a coded language that she doesn't understand.

This moment mirrored all these numerous moments before in the last few days, "Maybe this is normal, " she thought to herself trying not to give it more thought than it deserves.

## The Early Morning Hour That The Plan Takes Place

They are both standing just outside in the darkness, in the pitch blackness of the Police Station, the front side and turning around at the same time they wink at one another before they proceed into the Police Station.

"It's now or never," says Georgie to Jules and she nods smiling her golden smile that he felt brought him all kinds of luck.

## The Day After The Police Station Robbery

Jules tip toes into Georgie's room looking a little all over the place and quietly closes the door without a squeak or sound.

George watches her amazed that her fear has finally gotten the best of her.

"Jules.."

And at the sound of his voice she nearly jumps, "What's wrong with you?" he asks quietly as he watches her fidgeting on one foot and then the next and back on the first foot again.

Unable to even look at him Jules looks away.

"Nothing I'm just a little bit paranoid," she says stating the obvious.

"A little?" he asks giggling.

"Stop turning everything into a joke Georgie," she says fed up with his childish attitude.

"Jules we are fine, we didn't get caught last night, so what are you doing freaking out, you didn't even freak out before we went in and now you want to freak out after the whole thing?" he asks dismayed.

"It's just that – you know what happened just as we were about to leave …"

George interrupts her, "Yeah but we didn't leave in that second Jules so we're fine now, we left nearly an hour later, really it's over, we dodged that bullet nearly 24 hrs ago," he says softly to her just realizing how fragile she's become after last night's triumph.

Well in George's head it's a triumph because of the bag of clues they gathered in Sheriff Don's office and because of course they never got caught.

She looks at him and suggests watching her favorite TV episode like they used to in the old days, he immediately relents, anything is better than this.

### **A Few Days After**

### ***Bag of Clues:***

- *A navy blue glove – dirty with a little dirt and mud on its fingers (only one pair found in Sheriff Don's drawer).*

- *A photocopy of one dirty muddy footprint*

- *A metal key*

- *A screw and a bunch of nails in a plastic bag*

-*A shovel found hidden in one of his cupboards (the key found in one of his drawers opened the cupboard with the shovel).*

"Okay so when are we going to deal with the shovel?" asks Jules out of the blue one morning as she sits in Georgie's kitchen.

"Shovel? What do you have in mind Jules?" he asks relieved that she's finally herself again.

"Well I mean we took this big shovel and now its hiding in your dad's garden shed and what? Are we meant to just leave it there? Why did we take it then?" she said exasperated.

"Jules what do you want us to do with it? It's not like we can test it for finger prints."

"Well why not?" she asks naively.

"Jules it's been clearly cleaned properly so much so I can see my own face in it with every scratch and little spot that I have," he said again to Jules who's just refusing to listen to his logic about the shovel.

"We can't keep arguing about this shovel Jules," I say pleading with her to let it go for once and for all.

"Who's arguing Georgie, we are discussing," she points out.

"Okay we can't keep on discussing the same thing," he says growing agitated by the minute.

"Why the hell not?" she demands.

"Because we have other clues to figure out," he said as they both fell silent at once.

## **Two Weeks After**

"We need to figure out that photocopy of the muddy footprint that we found," he says reminding Jules of the necessary things to do.

"Oh, just let it go Georgie, we've tested everything else with the friend of yours that works in that lab in the next town over and remember what he said?" she asks.

"That we should stop coming to him with anything and everything and he's right we are reading too much into everything Georgie," she said calmly.

"But how about if we just try one last thing Jules, pretty please with a cherry on top," he pouts and turns to Jules trying to get her to drop her way of doing things just this once.

"Okay fine stop pouting like a baby girl, but really this is the last clue we test okay?" she said concluding their whole conversation.

## The Week After They Tested

"I can't believe it George, you were right," she says looking at me all wide eyed and shocked.

"I can't believe it myself either," I say waiting for the shocking feeling to subside but an hour later and it still hasn't.

"I can't believe that the muddy footprint is Jase's and I can't believe that Sheriff Don hid that clue from all of us," I say transfixed on the results that had just come in.

"Us? How about his parents Georgie?" she said looking even more shocked.

"Why would he do that and besides he's not the cautious intelligent detective type because when he found that red jumper in the ditch in the woods he didn't even have the intelligence to wait and find out if it belonged to Jase before he informed his whole family and look what happened after that," she said reminding me that Sheriff Don is as thick as a block of wood.

"So he does everything backwards?" I ask.

"He finds out that the footprint is Jase's and then decides to keep that evidence to himself hidden in another stupid description report about the location and finding of the muddy footprint?" I ask thinking how ridiculous he is and how stupid the whole police force is in this county to allow somebody of that caliber to join its forces.

"Where was it found again?" she asks thinking hard.

I reach into my pocket and take out a copy of the report and read it to her:

*"The footprint muddy in nature is found on a concrete slab on the corner of the road heading onto the highway bridge for the next town. The direction of the footprint would suggest that the defendant in question headed through the woods as a shortcut to get to this point and didn't take the pavement or the walking path as most pedestrians in this town do."*

"Don't read the rest, I feel like I've memorized it already," says Jules and just as I hear her admitting that – I realize that I feel exactly the same.

I walked around with Lucas that day, from the very early morning until late at night, past midnight late; Cinderella's carriage turned pumpkin late.

"Hey Georgie," said Lucas, with a quivering voice, almost too afraid to say the unthinkable.

"Yup Luke," I answered whimsically.

He turned to face me, facing away the city of lights below; New York City; the city of all cities.

"What's up?" I asked, not sure why he had suddenly gone rather quiet and distant. Considering only a few hours ago he was a bull bulldozing into the city, muscling his way in and out of every other corner.

But he didn't answer.

Maybe because he was distant.

He just walked away. It was hard that day to tell whether he was walking away from me, his friend, his all time buddy in the gang of adventure of the missing lad, or if he walked away from the truth that he had known.

It wasn't until I searched the rooftop endlessly for an hour and the grounds surrounding the building that I finally gave up and marched back home, took the train out of town and felt completely exhausted and drained.

I just couldn't imagine another missing buddy, Jason had gone missing nearly 6 months ago, to think that Lucas can too is just too much; it's unthinkable.

But then again had anyone turned around and told me a year back that Jase would go missing and that I'd start having feelings of love for Jules I'd think that they've gone mad, just insane!

And that happened.

Hours later I walked into my dad's lounge:

"Hi dad," I said.

He didn't even bother to look up from today's paper, although he was reading it past midnight so it's already yesterday's paper. Reading yesterday's paper today; that's how fast paced New York is. There just aren't enough hours in the day to do everything. The city is continuously spinning out of control and you with it.

"Dad?" I asked.

He looked at me and nodded for me to sit down next to him on the brown duty leather couch.

"I…I ….I…"

"You what kid?" he asked.

"I need to know the truth and I know you know it," I blurted it all out in a hurry as if I was petrified that my words could bite me in the ass had I said them slowly enough.

My dad's face weathered into a storm and just like that he turned back to his paper.

The headlines jammed in between his forehead, their words growing larger by the second.

He was feeling dizzy, just so dizzy.

"I'm feeling a little dizzy son, can this wait until tomorrow?" he stated as he unbuttoned his shirt and loosened his tie.

"No it can't."

He was surprised.

"It can't?" he asked looking confused.

"Yeah, it can't," I said forcing the issue.

He held his glass of whisky and took a sip of it letting it linger on his taste buds.

I waited and waited some more and noticed that my dad was getting rather uncomfortable in his own arm chair, his favorite beloved lounge that he spent endless number of hours in through the months and even years.

"Is it about Jase?" he asked feigning ignorance.

"Yes of course it is, who else could it be about!" I suddenly scream out loud, fed up with the way he was treating me.

"Come son, sit down here," he said ignoring my scream.

"I sat down next to him and as he grabbed my hand in his, I grew scared as I suddenly considered that the truth could be, the truth could be very bad.

"Dad, is it bad?" I asked becoming a kid all over again.

"Yes it is but ……..".

I interrupted him.

"I don't want to know, dad." I said cutting him off and immediately ceasing the moment to walk out of the lounge and straight into the safety of my room.

## **THE NEXT DAY**

I was back at dad's lounge the very next night. Again past midnight he was busy reading yesterday's paper and drinking whisky.

"Dad I must know the truth."

My dad just put down his paper, looked at me and said, "You're clearly not ready for the truth."

Just simply he had ended the conversation before it even began.

"But I am dad," I insisted.

"You see I thought yesterday that I wanted to know the truth but then when you told me that it's bad I just needed to run away. But I never really did run away even when I ran all the way into my room, I just couldn't get any sleep because……"

"Because Jase first went missing in your room."

"Yeah," I answered a little relieved that dad understood what I was trying to tell him.

"And I just couldn't sleep not even a wink all night and today I was in school half asleep like a zombie."

"Okay, but you really may not be ready to hear this, kiddo you sure you want to know this?"

I nodded.

"Because once it's done, it can't be undone."

I nodded again.

"Jase went to bed that night in your room and then got up to go to the bathroom."

I nodded for him to continue, afraid that he might continue.

"He stayed in the bathroom for much longer than you thought or any of us."

I nodded, listening and remembering how I had fallen asleep with my back to the door leaning on it with Timmy in my lap.

"He must have tripped in the bathroom over maybe a rumpled mat because we assume that his head must have hit the sharp edge of the sink as he fell to the floor and that's how he got knocked out, unconscious for hours."

He paused and took a gulp of his whisky.

"You must have fallen back to sleep because when you got up in the morning, you just somehow forgot to go and freshen up in your bathroom, maybe ……"

"Yeah, I got up and stared at the bed and when I didn't find him in the bed and the bed sheets on his side of the bed were all ruffled, I ran downstairs looking for him thinking that he was already up and eating his breakfast."

"Because that's the moment he was left alone in your bedroom."

My dad grew silent as the moments passed and the seconds ticked away.

"An hour later, or we assume that its much closer to a couple of hours later after you woke up at 9 am, nobody was in the house, we were all out."

"Wait dad, whose 'we', Sheriff Don?" I asked.

"No, the doctor that tended to his injuries."

I exhaled, feeling at once relieved, it sounded like he was alive after all.

"Dad, is he…?" I dared not finish my sentence.

Mr. Whitmore just walked up to his son and hugged him for all life's worth. Hoping to hug out all the pain that his words were about to inflict in his own son's heart.

I pulled away from dad.

My eyes filled up with hot tears and they started spilling down my cheeks.

"Now son, don't worry it's not as bad as we first thought."

His words cut through me like a sharp meat knife.

"What do you mean 'not as bad as we first thought?"

Is it possible that my dad had known all along and hid me away from what happened to my dearest buddy Jase. Dad interrupted my thoughts.

"Son, we couldn't tell you right away, we had to see how we should best handle it, the situation first, it's our responsibility."

"Dad stop this! It's not business, Jase was or is not a business deal he's a human being, he's my friend god damn it!"

I was charged up with anger, I could feel my veins in my neck almost pop out as my blood thickened in my veins and boiled.

I got up and ran again back to my room but this time my dad followed right behind me.

"Georgie! Stop wait you need to listen and hear the rest, this is only half the story!" he shouted at me, pleading for me to listen and stop jumping to conclusions.

But I just couldn't stop and listen and even locked myself in my bathroom escaping the end of the story, the end of Jase.

Dad kept knocking at the door, his fist pounded away for what seemed like an eternity and then silence.

## **THE DAY AFTER THE NEXT DAY**

I fell asleep in the bathroom that night but I slept well. Enough to not realize that ten hours had passed since I last heard dad knocking down my bathroom door.

But as I stood up my body ached all over, apparently cold tiles of the bathroom floor were not made with the idea that somebody would use them as a mattress.

I got into the shower and half an hour later got out of the bathroom, refreshed and got dressed up with a simple Levis and a white washed T-Shirt.

I walked downstairs hungry and only thinking of eggs or cereal for breakfast.

"Morning Dad," I quickly saluted him and got my cereal and bowl out of the cupboard and opened the fridge to get my milk out to prepare my quick breakfast.

"Well are we going to finish what we started last night or are you going to run away the minute you hear something that you don't like the sound of?" he asked me but his tone seemed rather sarcastic.

I just simply stared at him, gulping down the rest of my cereal in large mouthfuls.

Once I had finished munching on the last bite, I followed it with a sip of milk and walked out of the kitchen and out the front door.

I hadn't noticed dad's look, had I noticed it, I may have stopped in my tracks and begged him to continue the whole truth and nothing but the truth so help him god; but that would have happened only had I noticed and I hadn't.

The phone starts ringing uncontrollably off the hook and Mr. Whitemore thinks twice about answering. His gut feeling tells him that its bad news; but unlike his son, his years of experience give him the courage to get up and face his demons.

"Morning, Whitmore here," he answers in his business-like tone.

"Hi Sheriff, what can I do for you today?"

"No I haven't told him yet, I tried but……"

"I understand, I completely……"

"Yes the court date is round the corner, I'm aware of that."

He gently places the phone back on the hook and walks over to his study to look for Jase's file that Sheriff Don had given him months back. It was illegal to get confidential files out of the Department of Forensic Police Investigations but Don had made an exception, exception to the rule and Mr. Whitemore's gratitude to Sheriff Don is unmatched.

As he scanned through a stack of files in his personal filing cabinet, he laughed at himself, a sour laugh, a chuckle that left him breathless, almost choking on sobs and minutes later the great and all powerful Mr.Whitemore was left crying in his own pool of tears.

## **THE DAY AFTER THE NEXT DAY AFTER THAT DAY**

Georgie made a decision that day – a decision that took balls to make and loads of courage.

"Hey Jules, how about if I stay over tonight at your place, just right here," he said to Jules as he lay haphazardly on her bedspread and pointed at the bed, digging his finger into the mattress as he rolled over to Jules and started tickling her to death on her sides, forcing laughter to erupt from within her.

"Well, I guess…"

"You guess!" and with that he started tickling her again as they fell into each other's arms and rolled over together on the bed, Georgie on top of Jules.

He wanted her so much that night and he thought she probably did too but she was just not as certain about it as he was, but then again he was just assuming all this. And assumptions were sometimes not true and at others they were just that – full of truth.

He woke up the next morning and walked into Jules bathroom were he showered before he planted a simple kiss on her cheek as she still lay asleep in the land of her dreams. He left that morning without waking her up or telling her goodbye.

He did this because he cared so much for her that even saying goodbye to her for a short time would break his heart, this wasn't a girl he'd ever want to say goodbye to, this was a girl he wanted by his side permanently.

When he walked in that morning, he found his dad in yesterday's suit, lying face down in a file on his desk in the study in deep sleep and snoring like hell. It was obvious he had not changed or showered or even shaved for that matter and he had fallen asleep in the wee hours of the morning after working so hard as per the usual.

"Dad," said George.

"Wake up Dad," said George.

Mr. Whitemore got up, opened his eyes and saw a blurry version of his son standing in front of him in his lounge.

"Morning Kiddo," he said in a croaky voice.

Georgie nodded and walked into the kitchen, made him a ready-made cappuccino and walked back into the study and handed it to his dad expectantly.

"What is it son?"

"Dad, do you think…"

"It's not the right time kiddo, I'm barely half awake."

"Right dad," he said and walked out of his study unsure about much especially as he had noticed that the file his dad was buried in had Jase's name all over it.

What did dad know about Jase's disappearance and why was his file there? Dad was no cop.

He thought that it was time to go back to Jules place and wake her up, she could help him find some answers.

And that's exactly what he did.

## **THAT SAME DAY AT NOON**

"I don't know Jules; it just doesn't add up or make sense at all."

"Well maybe you read the name wrong Georgie on that file because Jase is all that's on your mind these days."

I wanted to tell her that it's not true that she was on my mind as much as Jase if not more but I couldn't. I just couldn't, I just wasn't ready to.

"What's dad doing with Jase's file Jules?"

"Why does he have it and why has Don…"

"If that's truly Jase's file then Sheriff Don has done something illegal Georgie by giving him that file."

"That's what scares me Jules, because if that's true then Sheriff Don is helping dad hide something or the reverse, dad helping Don hide something – either way you're right as it's against the law."

"Wanna have a break Georgie?"

Was she serious? Of course I wanted to have a break with her, who wouldn't?

"Sure Jules, let's go to the ice cream parlor."

"Sounds like a plan."

"Sure does," I said.

## **THAT SAME DAY IN THE AFTERNOON**

"Yummy it's a great flavor," I took a bit out of my ice cream cone and hummed a tune.

"Can I try Georgie?" asks Jules slyly.

"No you can't," says Georgie laughing at her as always.

"Oh come on give me a bite Georgie…"

"Nope aint gonna happen Jules," I laughed and thought how funny that a simple afternoon at the local town's ice cream parlor can make me this happy, so happy that I almost forgot for a simple second that Jase has been missing now for a good 6 months, 6 long months.

## THAT SAME DAY IN THE EARLY EVENING

## THAT SAME DAY IN THE EVENING

## THAT SAME DAY AT MIDNIGHT

## THAT SAME DAY PAST MIDNIGHT

It was all just a matter of time. The day seemed cut up into parts and every time, a little more time passes, the clearer things get.

"Jules," I whispered in her ear.

"Yeah," she said as she turned in her bed next to me.

"I think soon we will know everything. How Jason disappeared and why."

She smiled at me and kissed me on the lips for the first time.

"It's a matter of time." I said quietly shocked at her kiss and just as easily as that fell back asleep.

The next morning I woke up early, well earlier than her and watched her sleeping. Without any rhyme or reason I just planted a little peck on her lips and woke her up.

She smiled at me and grabbed me pulling me back into bed with her. She kissed me, a long hot lingering kiss and as I moved above her body in the bed I started kissing her neck slowly but surely feeling as if I had made all these moves before. They were all natural to me. And that's when I noticed that being with her was just soo natural.

I bit her ear and got out of bed.

"Hey where are you going Georgie?"

"I'm going to shower."

"Can I come with you?"

I could not believe my ears or my eyes as I watched her carefully get out of bed, stand and yawn and then walk past me into the bathroom, grabbing my hand in the process and getting me to follow her into the shower.

That's when I knew that girls called all the shots and guys like 'us' just followed them; if we were lucky and I am lucky today.

A smile so large hung on my face as if a hanger was permanently in my mouth.

When I saw her naked body under the shower I knew for certain that our friendship was ruined for good but oh my god what a body, what a beauty and what a start into adolescence.

If this is it, if this is all the confusion and anger and anxiety that clouds your mind through the thunderstorm lightning that others call – the teenage years – then I want nothing more than to re-live them over and over again.

This was all good – who am I kidding? This is great, even awesome! I thought to myself as I skipped back home, my head way up in the clouds or as the saying goes – in could 9.

I walked into the house and peered carefully into dad's lounge and that's when I saw a red handkerchief on his arm chair. A red handkerchief and that's all.

This house is beginning to sound like the setting of the legendary game – Cluedo, except there are no clues to find here; here you just read people's sleep patterns and facial reactions!

I walked on upstairs, suddenly feeling the turmoil pressure my shoulders, feeling like I was carrying a ton of bricks on them, I heaved myself up the stairs and into my room.

I stood above dad, towering above him as he just lay there, unmovable.

But I quickly learnt that he was sound asleep in my bed with his socks and shoes still on and his tie perfectly tied on his neck as if all he had to do is wear his jacket suit and he'd be ready to lead a conference team in a big corporation through the latest merger or acquisition.

Dad must have felt somebody stare at him because he suddenly fidgeted and opened the right eye forcing himself to wake up to his surroundings in my bedroom.

"Son, are you watching me sleep?" he asked slowly remembering how he had woken up in front of his desk in the lounge and found me ready with a cup of coffee.

"No dad, I'm waiting to see when is a good time to speak to you."

"And somehow you think that the best time to speak to me is when I'm asleep or have just woken up?"

As he mouthed those words my head jolted my memory back to the night that Jase slept over.

"Oh my god!" I screamed and ran to my drawer looking for the torch that Jas had woke me up with that night before he had disappeared.

But I couldn't find it anywhere.

As I emptied the drawer, all the magazines fell to the floor and my Playboy ones glared at my dad beside my feet.

"Son!" he scolded me.

"Is this what you're reading these days?"

"Yeah because that's what's important here." I said rather quietly and discreetly.

And just as suddenly I froze and turned around to face my dad.

Looking at my dad, tears stung my eyes as the missing memory of Jase waking me up using a torch and shinning it first in my face and then in his face came back to haunt me.

He said something after he shined the torch on his own face but I just couldn't get my head round it. So I bought time and questioned my dad on the things that made absolutely zero sense to me.

"What's up with that red jumper that Sheriff Don found that day when we thought the worst had happened to Jase and then it turned out to belong to someone else entirely?"

"And what's up with that red handkerchief that is downstairs on your arm chair in the lounge?"

"Dad, what the heck is going on?"

My father just turned away and fell back asleep in my bed, leaving me in more wonder than when I had first entered my house; my parents house.

An hour later I woke up dad as I tugged on his sleeve asking, almost pleading with him to give me all the answers, the right ones, to take me back to that horrifying night and to tell me in detail what had happened:

"Even if it's bad dad, its time I know, don't you think?" I asked him, remembering at the same time to be careful what I wish for.

"Dad I remember, I remember the last thing that Jase said to me before he disappeared that night," I said quietly to dad almost afraid I was going to wake up the ghost.

**"Sleep-over time,"** I murmured to myself before saying it out loud for dad to hear.

"Okay son here's what happened":

"That morning when you woke up and went downstairs to the kitchen to look for Jase, he was already knocked out unconscious on the floor of your bathroom probably from falling and hitting his head against the sharp edge of the sink. After you left the house and we were already out, the house was empty; Jase woke up with a thumping hard headache. His head felt like it had been smashed into bits. He managed to stumble clumsily out of the bathroom and down the stairs.

He must have grabbed your red jumper from your chair that morning feeling that he could get cold and need it outside to wear. That's the same jumper that was found in the ditch in the woods on the outskirts of our local town. At first Sheriff Don thought that this clue was as clear cut as daylight; the jumper belonged to Jase and the fact that it was found after he went missing and found in the location of a ditch in the woods on the outskirts of our local town would suggest that he could be dead or even worse being tortured day in, day out by a captive."

I looked at dad petrified.

"But then Sheriff Don took the red jumper and had it cross tested and examined in a lab, the DNA particles in a little hair strand embedded in the red jumper belonged to you. That's right none other than you and the finger prints were both yours and his. So he came to see me after he spent a night toying with possibilities and decided in the morning just to pass by my office and have a chat with me; just to clarify things. We got together that morning and I was just shocked, I just couldn't believe what he was telling me and so when he showed me the evidence I grew reluctant to help him or even listen to him."

Mr.Whitemore walks over to his son and grabs his hand placing it in his.

"Son, I want you to know, need you to know that I knew you had nothing to do with Jase's disappearance but I also knew that there could be a possibility that if Jase's body was ever found in future and if they needed to desperately close the case and punish someone for the crime, anyone close enough to the crime and with evidence – you'd be the one they'd choose without even blinking an eye."

Mr. Whitemore looked away as he walked towards the window and stood there, his back to his son, making what he had to say next, all that much easier.

"Dad," I croaked.

"You thought I did it?" I croaked as pain filled my voice with despair.

"No son, I did not," said his dad not even bothering to turn around and face him.

"So?" I asked.

"Well, that's why I demanded to keep Jase's file with me, locked in my office safe until I figured out a way out of this mess."

"But why would you keep it with you if you were sure that I had nothing to do with it?" I asked as I realized that his statements were not really adding up.

"Because I needed to make sure that you're in the clear."

Mr.Whitemore turned around and finally faced his son.

"In the clear?" I croaked.

"What does that mean?" I asked bewildered.

"It means, son, that I had a little doubt that's all but most of all I didn't trust Sheriff Don and that's why I kept the file."

"So why were you looking at it a couple of nights ago?" I asked quietly.

"What? When?" he asked with innocence as he had clearly forgotten.

"When I woke u up with a cappuccino that morning and your face was buried in Jase's file on your desk in the lounge, remember?" I said.

"Oh that, well when you came in a few nights ago and suddenly asked out of the blue about Jase and demanded to know, knowing very well that I knew, you made it sound like somebody had told you part of the story but refused to tell you the whole of it and so you came to me to find out the rest. I wanted to protect you…"

"Protect me, from what?" I asked thinking how ridiculous this all sounded.

"Protect you from you finding out 2 things: that for one minute it seemed like you had a hand in Jase's disappearance and the second thing that I did not want you to find out exactly what actually happened to Jase because it could pain you afterwards for a long time."

He went on: "By the time I was 100% sure that you had nothing to do with it, I needed to protect you from the awful truth of what did happen to Jase and what the doctor finally diagnosed after examining him and doing a range of tests."

Mr. Whitemore swallowed hard; coughing to clear his throat he looked at me and told me the truth.

"Jase wanted a simple sleep-over that's all but instead he fell, hit his head, knocked himself unconscious for most of the night until he suddenly woke up in your bathroom and stumbled out looking for you or even us, anybody in the family or in this house. He couldn't find anyone and so left and decided to go to the nearest hospital in the local town and get himself tested because his head felt like it was going to explode all over the sidewalk. And somehow and we still don't quite know how he ended up in the Wilshire Memorial Hospital on the outskirts of our local town. There he ran all the tests and found out that he …."

"Wait, how do you explain the red handkerchief?" I asked challenging him.

"What red handkerchief?" he asked dismayed.

"The one downstairs in your chair."

I found myself alone in my room as dad ran downstairs to see what I was on about.

He came back laughing and showed me how the handkerchief is a tiny one that fits inside the front upper right hand pocket of his jacket suit; as a little red contribution to his navy blue red suit.

"The doctor found out that Jase's head is not as well adjusted as we had both hoped. He noticed a little incision just above his right ear and found out that's where he must have fallen and first hit his head but I later found out that a permanent memory loss is a direct result of being knocked out unconscious for a few hours – parts of the brain had less oxygen than others and we were lucky…"

"Lucky?!" I screamed at dad.

"Yes, lucky that he did not lose much other than parts of his memory; he could have had parts of his brain that were brain damaged – if absolutely no oxygen gets to the brain for a number of hours then that part will be declared brain dead."

Mr.Whitemore looked at me and said, "So that's what happened, Jase is not dead nor injured but he's working on dealing with what happened to him and trying to get his memory loss back."

"So what's that got to do with me? Why didn't you tell me and how come none of my friends in my gang know?" I asked as I noticed how much I've been kept out of the loop so far.

"Lucas knows but felt that it's more appropriate to tell you himself but he couldn't do it, he tried tonight but it just didn't work, the rest of course have no idea yet."

"So why didn't you tell us so that we can at least visit him and I could've stopped having nightmares in my bedroom?"

"I couldn't tell you, I'm sorry, there's far too much at stake," he walked over to me and told me that Jase, Jason woke up not remembering me as his friend or anybody from that gang at all.

And that's when I remember crying – for how long I wept I cannot remember but looking back on it now, I remember my vow not to live except day by day and take everything in my life with a pinch of salt.

A few hours later and as fatigue ate through my bones I fought with my eyelids not to sleep but before I knew it, I was deep asleep and in my bedroom.

### **The Morning After I Found Out**

I woke up and for the first time in a very long time I felt well and deeply rested. I smiled because Jase is not dead, maybe the old Jase is but really he's not dead just his memory is.

And I smiled an even larger smile when I thought of Jules and the afternoon before I found out about Jase. Who wouldn't smile about that?

And as I turned on my side to snuggle more into my bed, I saw Timmy sleeping in my bed over my duvet.

I knew that these days were numbered; the days were you felt like the whole world was working with you and for you.

My mobile phone rang off into the distance and I answered it.

"Heya Jules.."

"I have something to tell you…"

"What? What do you mean? What court date? For what?"

I closed the phone and rushed into the bathroom to get ready and go meet Jules. There was much more to the story than I have been told.

In anger I threw on anything reasonable and ran out of my room and minutes later out of my house and hurried down the road.

A few minutes later I opened my front door again and peered my head into my house and called out to Timmy to join me – in my hurry out of the house I had forgotten my best ally – my good old Timothy.

Seconds later he barked and ran outside the front door to greet me.

"Timmy you good old fella, such a great friend, always by my side, full of fun and – of Timmy stop it, stop it …" I said as he jumped over me and started licking me, "I'm happy to see you to."

**The Noon After I Found Out**

"Come in George," said Jules calmly.

She is eerily calm as she holds the door open for me.

"Jules," I say inhaling as I feel rather exasperated.

"Calm down Georgie," she says her voice barely a whisper.

"What's wrong Jules?" I ask as she looks at me with those eyes; the same ones that she uses when she gets a little uncomfortable – the ones just before a thunderstorm.

"Nothin,' she says as she walks to the kitchen counter and pours herself an orange juice. As she starts drinking it, I watch her thinking of her calmness that is so uncharacteristic of her.

"So?" she asks as she wipes her mouth clean.

"What about the court date?" I ask wondering why dad always leaves bits and pieces out.

"Well, I heard my mama talking about it the other day on the phone. She seemed so wrapped up in the matter that she didn't notice me standing behind her."

"So what did you hear?" I asked.

"Well I think that she's hiding something with your dad but I'm just not sure what it is."

"Hiding something? Like what Jules?"

"I'm not sure but we have to find out Georgie because she's acting a little odd."

I walk over to Jules and at once remember that I haven't told her about our buddy Jase and I start fidgeting on one foot as I ponder how to tell her.

"What's wrong Georgie?" she asks as she points to my shivering left leg.

"Jules I know – I mean I just found out what happened to Jase that night…" my voice trails off into the distance and I'm left speechless.

"Okay," she says as her pupils grow larger by the second in intrigue.

"Jase is not dead but he's as good as dead to us," I say as I let my words fall onto Jules and wait for her reaction.

"What???!" she screeches.

"Jules he's well and alive but.."

"But what Georgie, what?!" she asks as anger becomes one with her.

"But because he hit his head on my sink in the bathroom and fell unconscious for a few hours, he suffered brain injuries that have left him intelligent but he lost some of his memory."

"Memory loss," she asks as her eyes fill up with tears threatening to spill over her cheeks and land on her beautiful light pink blouse.

"Yup, that's why he's dead to us.."

She interrupts me, "Stop saying that, he's not dead to us, he's just forgotten us – that's all."

I walk over to Jules and hug her, she pulls away from my embrace and at once I get it. Today I'm the bearer of bad news and that's all there was to it.

## That Same Afternoon

We are back on the lake.

I watch as Jules walks beside me not saying a word and I look across at the lake and notice the sun setting as it reflects the light over the darkest of its waters.

"Jules?" I ask trying again to talk to her for like the millionth time.

She doesn't answer and the worst part in all of this? I really don't know when she will answer me.

We walked side by side for nearly an hour before she:

"Georgie, I am sorry but I'm just so angry at Jase. I'm angry at him stumbling over something and ruining our memories, I'm angry at the time of fear and anxiety we spent wondering what had happened to him, I'm angry that before he left us – he never gave us a chance to say goodbye but most of all I'm angry that I feel this way – I'm blaming him for something he has nothing to do with – it's not his own doing because accidents do happen-you know."

"I'm angry because I feel guilty."

"I know Jules, I'm angry that Lucas knew before we did and never had the courage or balls to tell us, I'm angry because we can't just call up Jase and ask him to join us at the lake like always."

We both walked on unsure what the future held –

### That Same Evening

We both sat down at the dinner table unsure what the present held.

Later that evening as we sat down with her mum and aunt in the living room watching a re-run of a

TV episode, we realized how unsure we are even about the past.

And as I walked back home, Timmy by my side, I watched him bark at the shinning moon that hung in the serene night sky and I hoped that one day I'd have the courage to yell at Lucas for what he had not said and that's when I knew: that day isn't any closer.

But as my head met the pillow that night, I remembered that I still had no idea about 'the court date,' and Jules mum's hidden agenda with my dad.

## The Only Morning After Our Doubts

I woke up with a banging – a constant loud banging on the front door. By the time I opened my eyes and stumbled down the stairs to the front door and opened it, his back was already to me as he started walking away, down the front steps.

I called after that fool.

"Sheriff wait!" I yelled at him, watching him disappear further into the distance.

"Wait, why are you running away from me!" I yelled at the top of my lungs so that he can hear me.

That's when he stopped and turned to face me.

He frowned, "Why don't you ask your dad that?" he said, his tone strong and solid.

I closed the front door and ran upstairs to search for my mobile phone.

Finding it I punched in the numbers one by one and held my breath as I heard the dial tone in my ears.

"Mr. Whitemore here," said an all too familiar voice.

"Dad," I said quietly.

"Yes son."

"Dad, why didn't you tell me about Sheriff Don?"

I waited for his reply but never got anything but grunting down the line.

"What about him?"

I knew my dad was playing dumb; he's easy to read even over the phone.

"Dad please you know exactly what it's about," I pleaded with him to stop those games; I was truly fed up of him playing games with me.

"Son there isn't much to tell, I already told you about Jason's file that I kept in my safe in the lounge."

"No dad you didn't, you just told me what you had to tell me because I caught you with your head fast asleep on top of his file," I reminded him.

"Son, what are you trying to get at?"

"That you hid something from me once before so you could just as easily be hiding something from me now again but this time you have no reason to tell me, not yet anyway."

I exhaled and sat down on my bed, lying all the way down on my back and facing my ceiling.

"Son, this is no way to speak to your father."

"Dad please just for once tell me what the heck is going on."

"There isn't anything."

His words sounded absolute and final.

"Dad Sheriff Don came to see you today."

"What?"

"He knocked on the door and by the time I answered it, he started walking away from me not wanting to see or talk to me, I had to call after him."

And dad still said nothing.

"I asked him why is he running away from me and he said that I should ask you that. So now I'm asking."

"Dad?" "Dad?"

But dad was gone and in his place he had hung up the phone.

I got up and threw the phone on my duvet in anger.

My face red and hot, I couldn't handle many more surprises than that. God only knows what's gotten into him now.

## The Minute He Walked In

I was fast asleep on the living room couch watching a movie when my dad suddenly walked in and switched off the TV. I woke up the second the TV went mute.

"Oh, hi," I said grudgingly.

"Son, get up and wash your face, we need to have a talk."

"Dad I'm sleepy I want to continue sleeping for a little bit."

"Son, you asked a question and now come and here it's answer."

"Ok dad what's going on?"

"It's simple really, sheriff Don needs Jason's File back and I refused to give it to him."

"But why dad?" I asked a little confused. I just couldn't figure dad out these days.

"Because until Jason regains his full memory I don't think I should hand his file back to the police. God knows what they will do with it."

"Dad what are you afraid of?"

"Son sometimes a little precaution is necessary and that doesn't mean you're in fear of something," he explained.

"But dad…"

"Go to bed son now and relax, you're in good hands and stop jumping to all kinds of conclusions just like that, rest now and then wake up and turn over a new leaf – a new page."

"But.."

"No buts just do as you're told."

And with that I vowed never to share much with my dad again, a conversation is a two-way street and so is trust and I knew then that I could never trust him again.

### Back To Jules

"So what about the court date?"

I asked Jules as I was busy eating my cheese and tomato sandwich the next afternoon.

"Georgie it's just something that my mum is involved in that's all."

I stopped munching my sandwich and looked up at her.

"What do you mean?"

"Do you know what it is?"

I told you before that I keep catching her chatting to your dad quietly, whispering things to him but I'm not too sure what it's all about.

"Okay Jules, how do you think we can find out?"

"Well come over in the mornings because she's always speaking to your dad on the phone then."

**That Next Morning**

"Shhh, I'm trying to listen Georgie please be quite."

I held the rest of my words in my mouth and sulked. Jules was taking this far too far already. We've been more than ten minutes trying to hear something, anything but still nothing.

"Shhhh," she scolded me quietly.

"What, I'm not even saying anything now."

"The 29th April -----of course I won't forget that date Jack, okay until then, see you, goodbye."

"Okay now we know that the court date is on the 29th of April," said Jules facing me again and removing her ear from up against the column of the white door and porcelain sculpture of a flying bird on the right next to the main mantle piece.

"Jules, how do we know that the 29$^{th}$ is the court date and not something else?"

"We're guessing Georgie," she answered quickly.

"Okay," I said.

"Okay," she said and with that we went in to the living room and continued to watch a TV sitcom that we both liked.

"Hey Jules, what's up with Lucas, have you spoken to him lately?" I asked her suddenly in the middle of our TV watching time.

"Not now George," she said impatiently.

"No, now Jules," I answered just as impatient.

"What is it George, what now?" She asked in an irritable tone.

"Have you heard from Lucas?" I repeated.

"Hhhhmmm yeah he called me – was it yesterday evening or the night before just to say hi, why?" she asked as she peered at my face closer.

"What you up to now?"

"Nothing Jules, can't I ask a question just like that?"

She looked at me a couple of seconds longer, lingering on my face as if she was busy studying it and then shrugged her shoulders and started watching TV again.

I really wanted to tell Jules why I cared if Lucas has been in touch with her or not but I just didn't think it's the right time to dive into this, she's already very irritable and her constant glares in my direction remind me how annoyed she is still with me for telling her the truth about jase's disappearance that night.

So I decided to do what I did best, ignore everything that had happened since that hateful night when he disappeared, even the good stuff like me and Jules sharing intimate moments together. I grew tired and restless from trying my best to work everything out – to figure out how and when it would all fall into place. So dad asked me to change over into a new leaf – and for the first time in my life I'm going to do just that – maybe there is wisdom in it. I've been a rebel without a cause for far too long. My head was spinning with so many thoughts and I felt a little tad bit scattered.

When the episode ended Jules came next to me and said:

"Georgie let's go and ask mum what's going on."

"Yeah right because she's just going to volunteer the truth to you."

"Why don't we just try first and see?"

"Okay," I said standing up and grabbing her by the hand and off the couch, "Let's go then and talk to her now."

She got up and we walked down the corridor and out by the porch and saw her mum standing and just looking into the distance, onto the road and garden ahead of the house.

"Mum hiya," said Jules as she walked up to her mum and kissed her cheek.

"Hi dear and hi George how are you today?" she asked in a polite but overtly formal tone.

"I'm good Mrs Smith."

"Mum we need to know what is going on with that court date?"

Her mum stares at us, her eyes large and a grin plays on her cheeks, she even looks a little blushed.

"How did you find out about that?" she asks us.

"Mum don't get mad but we overheard you talking to Georgie's dad in the morning and heard something about 29$^{th}$ April as THE court date."

Jules stopped talking and noticed her mum's expression coming alive with happiness.

"Oh, so it's not something bad that court date, right?" I asked after looking at her mum.

"Okay we really wanted to wait until the whole tragic episode with Jason blows over before we sit you both down and tell you."

She looked at me and Jules and smiled and said, "George, your father and I have decided to get married and the court date refers to the day we actually tie the knot."

I held my stomach and ran to the bathroom indoors and started vomiting in the sink. My head beat down on its shoulders and I felt dizzy and so disgusted with finding out that Jules who I love and who I've made out with will soon become my step sister!

Jules ran in after me and stood with the bathroom door open staring at me and silently crying and her mum followed us both just staring at us from the living room looking a little perplexed at our reactions.

"Kids I thought you'd be happy that you're going to be related, step sister and brother after all you're always together like best friends, shouldn't this be something you're both happy and excited about?"

Her mum's voice in the distance was all I could bare. I wash up and brush my teeth, freshen up and come out to see Jules hug me whispering in my ear, "Don't worry I still love you both ways."

How sad that the first time I hear her telling me how much she loves me is after I find out that she will be my step sister soon and won't be able to love me the way she does this instant.

This has got to be the drama that people talk about when they refer to the teenage years – and just like that I'm upset that I'm 13 years old and just wish I was back at being 12 or 11 years old when things in life were a lot less complicated and when Jules was just a best friend.

An hour later I go and find my dad as per the usual in his lounge and say, "You just had to do it, didn't you? You just had to decide to marry Jules's mum, just so that you can screw up the only good thing in my life right now!" I screamed at him and without noticing his shocked look, did what I always do best, walk away from my dad in anger, away from his stupid lounge, in this god forsaken stupid house.

A second later I walk back in and scream, "Just because mum is dead doesn't mean that you should remarry after 5 years! And look who you've chosen! My god you should be ashamed about how you behave and what you do, I'd be ashamed about it, and actually I wouldn't know where to hide my face!"

"Son, calm down Martha just called me and told me how both you and Jules are quite upset at finding out about us, let's have a chat," he said calmly unsure about whether this reaction from his son is because his son is afraid that his dad would love his mum any less or because of something else. But something in Mr.Whitemore knew that this wasn't the right time to push his son for more information or interrogate him.

After all his son just found out about his buddy Jase, Sheriff Don and now his dad's secret relationship with his best friend's mum.

So that's why Mr.Whitemore walked away and walked into the kitchen to make a cup of coffee, leaving a steaming, hot headed George behind.

"Dad," I said about half an hour after my outburst.

My dad didn't even look up from the book he is reading.

"Dad, it's not that I don't want you to be happy – it's just that I want to be happy too – it's not fair that –"

"Son life's unfair but what's gotten into you lately?"

I look at my dad and go over to him and give him a quick awkward hug.

"Dad I – I – I –"

"You what son?" he asks looking deep into my eyes wishing that he could read my somewhat troubled mind.

I turned my back to him and said it: "I love Jules dad and you marrying her mum will stand in my way and the thing is that she loves me too and …"

My dad puts his hand on my shoulder, giving it a squeeze, says, "Son I'm sorry I had no idea at all, does Martha even know this?"

His voice is as quite as a whisper now and his tone is full of emotion, I start thinking that it's sympathy in his voice, sympathy for me, sympathy for the way things are turning out for me but I am mistaken because:

"Son, it's not as bad as you think, you see you won't be her real brother, you will become her step brother that's all so you're not bound by anything …"

"But dad if I continue with her and you marry Martha won't it be like committing incest?"

I felt relieved that for the very first time I was letting dad into my world and letting him know my fears.

"Son," he smiled and at once I became relieved that perhaps I had misunderstood it all.

"Son, is that why you're in such a bad mood? You think you're about to commit incest?"

"Son come here, what incest?" he chuckled as he hugged me hard and patted me on the back from man to man.

"Son don't worry your little mind about that."

"But.."

"No buts because it's nothing like this, don't be silly it's not incest and will never be such a thing."

As an afterthought he pauses and asks me as his face looks rather concerned, "Son is that what Jules thinks too?"

"Yes she cried when she found out dad."

"Okay I am going to go right now to see Martha and see how best to handle this situation, don't worry son, all will be sorted out soon, go to bed, it's 2 am and I will speak to you tomorrow morning at breakfast."

I turned around to face the door and leave and smiled at dad and said, "Dad I love you, you know."

"I know son, I know that you do, I do too."

I climb into bed that night feeling both exhausted with the sudden news and relieved all at once so much so that my head hits the pillow and I sleep immediately.

## That Night With Martha

"Hi Todd, come in darling."

"Hi Martha," says Todd Whitemore as he quickly pecks her lips and walks into the house at 230am.

"Look sweetheart, I just spoke to George and he's quite cut up about us getting married and it's because he just opened up to me and told me that he's in love with Jules and that she loves him too, he's actually worried that he could be committing incest."

Martha starts laughing uncontrollably, "So that's why Jules has been locked away in her bedroom since she found out and George left, I tried to talk to her but she just keeps sobbing."

"I know it's not that funny but think about it from their perspective, they must have been petrified Toddy."

"Well now Georgie is much better because I explained everything to him and he's relieved but I'm just worried about Jules."

"Don't worry darling, I will talk to her first thing in the morning and Toddy, do we know how advanced their relationship is now?"

"What do you mean sweetheart?"

"As in do you think they are having sex?"

Martha suddenly looked tired and extremely worried as she toyed with such an implication in her mind.

"Martha, don't think this way, it will drive both of us crazy, they are too young, I mean Georgie is only 13 years old and your daughter is of the same age, it's ridiculous, I bet that all they've done is kiss and make out."

"I certainly hope so darling, I really do."

"In any case speak to Jules in the morning and as my son is more forthcoming with information, I will talk to him at breakfast and try to get to the bottom of whether they've had sex but darling I highly doubt it."

"Nighty then sweetheart and I hope to god you're right."

Todd kisses his fiancé goodbye leaves and walks home with a new found worry on his mind. Really sometimes it just feels like Georgie is testing his limits with him, he's such a hard kid to figure out.

## The Breakfast With Georgie

"Morning Son, I'm just going to go straight to the point, did you sleep with Jules?"

My son who had just poured himself a glass of cold milk dropped it to the floor sending the glass and its contents all over the floor.

"Dad, what you talking about? No I haven't had sex, why?"

"Son tell me the truth, don't worry I'm not going to scold you but I need to know now."

"Dad honestly I haven't had sex, why is that what Jules's mum thinks?"

"Are you sure son?" he asked one last time in an attempt to get the truth out into the open.

"Okay son then what have you done so far?"

"Dad that's private."

"Not when you're both under 16."

"Okay we've just made out, kissed and had a shower together, that's all I promise."

"Okay son but you really should realize that sex is not for you at this age, you need to first mature and then have sex responsibly."

"Dad I'm mature but when I have sex …"

Mr.Whitemore interrupted him, "When you are ready to have sex please come to me and tell me, I will advise you accordingly."

"Okay dad, is Jules in a lot of trouble now?"

"No she's not but son please respect the intimate times you've had together and keep them to yourself."

"Dad what happened last night when you went over there?"

"Jules was asleep but her mum was up in worry because Jules hadn't told her what happened between you both, she just locked herself in her room and cried, shutting her mum out."

"Dad are we both in trouble?"

"No not anymore because you acted responsibly by telling me what you did and confiding in me, son always do that and I can protect you."

"Okay dad," I said as I poured myself another glass of cold milk and started gulping it down.

"Hi darling, yes it's Toddy, don't worry they haven't had sex, just making out, yes I'm quite sure…" said Mr.Whitemore unaware that his son was busy hiding behind the door and listening to him.

## After That Breakfast

"Jules do you want to go out for a walk in let's say 10 mins?" I asked her on the phone.

"Okay that's great, see you then," I said as I hung up the phone and went upstairs to change into the new t shirt that she bought me a few days ago.

### After That Walk With Jules

I went back home and ran into the living room and jumped onto the couch. Timmy right by my side came over to me and laid his head in my lap.

That walk with Jules was great but better yet when we both decided to take matters into our own hands.

### After They Both Decided To Take Matters Into Their Own Hands

I stood beside Jules in the lobby of the Wilshire Memorial Hospital.

"Jason Donnahue is in room 352, down the hall, turn right, take the lift up to the $3^{rd}$ floor and there it will be, the door on your second left," said the hospital administrator with a growing smile.

I walked into the room with Jules and just found Jason in the middle of drawing in a notepad, oblivious of us both as we entered his room.

"Hey Jase," I said smiling a little afraid that he may be much worse than either of us had expected.

"Hi – sorry who are you?" he asked as his face turned blank as he stared at us both.

A few minutes later and Jules spoke up, "Jase don't you remember, I am your friend Jules and this," she said as she pointed at me, "this is your closest buddy George."

"I'm sorry but I really can't remember you guys but I guess you're right and besides I can't remember much those days since I woke up here, I mean that's what the doctors and my parents are telling me."

He looked away, the hollow physical shell of a boy they once knew and both loved.

## **1 YEAR LATER**

"I'm coming down dad!" I screamed at the top of my lungs.

I was in my room as always grabbing the first shirt and blue jeans that I could see in my packed and chaotic, messy closet.

"George, they're here, come down now!" screamed his dad at the head of the staircase.

I jumped into my jeans and yanked on the pink striped shirt and just ran downstairs almost tripping on Timmy in the doorway.

He barked at me his disapproval and I laughed patting his head lovingly and ran down the stairs.

"Dad, what is it, I'm…"

"Look whose here son," said my dad with the largest grin on his face and this man doesn't smile at all, even when he's at his happiest.

I stopped short when I saw Jules just standing in the entrance of my house with her mum Martha.

"Hi Gerogie," she said just as if I had last seen her yesterday at the hospital and not almost a year ago to that very day.

"Hi Jules," I said and walked to her side and just stared at her. If it was at all possible she even looked so much more beautiful than she had a year ago.

"Martha," said my dad dragging Martha by the hand into the living room, "Let's leave the kids alone, I bet they have a whole lot to catch up on."

"Sure Toddy," she said and smiled blushing in the process for she had not called him that since they had last set eyes on each other nearly a year ago as well. The memories of her and him, him and her were beginning to flood back into their minds as they made a conscious effort on both of their parts to leave the kids alone.

"So Georgie, you look a lot taller and a little older," smiled Jules, as if saying that was the most natural thing in the world.

I, of course still held a grudge, even a year later.

"Jules I can't…"

"Can't what?" she asked looking puzzled as if I was truly alone in the hurt of her ditching me, ditching us a year ago.

"Don't you remember how you ditched 'us' after the hospital visit just because it all hurt just too much to see Jase? You ditched me for Jase, remember Jules?" I asked snickering at her.

"How could I forget," she croaked as tears filled her eyes.

I was still hurt and pretty upset by the way she had ended things but I just didn't think she could still be hurt or even hurt at all since she was the one that ditched 'us' in the first place.

"You're upset?" I asked totally amazed.

"Of course I am Georgie."

"But why Jules?"

"Because I never wanted it to end, that's why."

I looked at her, my best friend in so many of my early years, my first love and also the woman who had broken my heart the first time I had discovered what a heart is and how to use it.

"I'm sorry Georgie, I really didn't want to hurt you or me or end it, I'm so sorry," she walked over to me and hugged me crying hot tears as they spilled on my newly fresh pink stripped shirt.

I pulled her away from me and just didn't know what to do. Who could?

# **2 YEARS LATER**

"We are 16 years old Jules!" I call to her from the other side of my new apartment as I show her around it.

"Yeah but isn't it a little too early for you to move out, it's not like you're 18, Georgie."

"Whatever Jules, stop being such a smart ass!" I laugh and stick out my tongue at her in the process.

"I'm not, I'm just saying that.."

We are both interrupted as the doorbell rings and I walk over to the door and open it to find one of the biggest surprises of my life just standing outside it.

"Hey George, I missed you man," he says and as he peers in through the door and sees Jules he adds, "Jules you too, god have I missed you both."

We both stand there in shock as we feel a ghost of the past is haunting us in the new flat; a friend, an old buddy, one of my closes friends – Jason.

Suddenly he pulls out a torch, lights it up and says, "Hey Georgie its Sleep-Over time," and just like that we are back in my old bedroom, in my old house just before he had disappeared and before I had lost my old friend Jase.

The best things in life come to those who wait and whether I had waited or not, whether Jules had waited or not, enough time had passed and Jase was back, not in the hollow physical shell of a boy we once knew but the old Jase.

The old Jase had returned and after we had spent nearly a whole day listening in excruciating wonder at the tale – his missing tale and his recovery, we realized the most important thing: Sometimes when things look so bad and they really are, sometimes if you're lucky enough you get another chance to start right where you first left off.

For me that was in a sleep over, in my bedroom, angry at Jules that had stolen my antique comic – The Hulk and Timmy, my old Timmy who had appeared in my youth, my pre-puberty years and who had disappeared when I turned 15 years old, my special friend Timothy the dog.

The most faithful dog anybody could ever have. A very friendly dog – clever, affectionate and loyal to me in particular; he provided me with physical and emotional protection.

I just adored him until one day I started to adore someone else.

# **HERE'S HOW IT HAPPENED**

I walk down the streets of the old suburban town and I meet Jules on the way just by the bookstore that we used to spend hours in and many endless summer afternoons.

"Hey Jules, where is the whole gang?"

She looks at me blankly.

Even Timmy starts barking getting impatient with Jules just as much as I.

"Well Lucas is down by the lake, along with Nancy, Derek and Lucy."

"Okay then let's get going," I say smiling at her.

"Okay then but let's go past the Ice Cream Parlor – it's a short cut that way."

"Okay Jules come on, come on Timmy you too," I say to both of them and start heading there.

As we near the Ice Cream Parlor I notice that Timmy is just lurking around my legs – he does that just before something big happens – I knew that he was trying to tell me that something is up or about to happen soon.

I smile at him and start patting him on the head and he barks in response to me. Just as I pass the window of the Ice Cream Parlor, I notice my reflection in the parlor's window and my hand is reflected as it is patting Timmy's head but …….

My hand is in fact patting nobody, its patting the thin air!

I jolt and stop abruptly just outside the window and stare at myself.

Just as Jules catches up with me I suddenly find the courage to hold her hand and drag her over the mini bridge and round to the lake.

"Thanks Timothy – you told me to expect something by lurking by my legs and you gave me enough courage to realize that I must after all those years that have passed re-kindle my relationship with the only woman I have ever loved, my first love, my best friend – my Jules."

So I grabbed her hand that day but at the same time I let go of Timmy's hand – my special invisible friend that was a dog, that was a shield against all life's greatest of challenges, life's greatest obstacles, life at its hardest – when a baby turns from a boy into a man, but before that turns into a teenager.

I tell you all, all the sad readers that are sad because Timothy never existed, or all the readers that think they are better than me and can do it all better and without Timmy's help, you just don't know what it's like to have someone like him around and undoubtedly no one will ever know – in fact no one ever knew, except and as she squeezed my hand as it lay in hers and winked at me – except Jules of course.

Now that's gotta be something!

# How They Did It – Broke Into The Police Station – Years Ago

"We need to wait here Jules just as if we are on a regular shift and out for a chat and a cigarette break in between work," I say looking at her and urging her to calm down because now is really not the time to start getting all nervous.

"I know we are Gerogie, we're supposedly cleaners on the night shift and look where we're standing right outside the front of the Police Station," I say reminding him that we are doing every step of the plan as we arranged.

"We need to stay here for like 15 minutes because we need to look like we have nothing to hide," I say.

Jules just nods away trying not to let the cigarette smoke bother her so much as she is under disguise.

"Remember," says Georgie as he throws his cigarette on the ground and puts it out with his shoes, like they both practiced taking tips from the movie Grease and the main last song and dance when the woman puts out her cigarette and starts dancing with the man, her partner.

"You are Mary and I'm Shane," he says slowly making sure that they've covered everything before they do what they came here to do.

He looks at her one last time and winks at her and in just the same moment she does the same winking at him.

They both go into the Police Station, walking into the reception and both go to the toilet – the men's toilet for Georgie and the ladies toilet for Jules were they both remain for a full 5 minutes before exiting carefully to avoid the CCTV two angled cameras on each corner above either toilet. The minute the camera's angle changes in the opposite direction, they make a run for it and head down the stairs all the way to the basement and then continue running all the way into the Storage Room.

There they stay for a full hour waiting for the main Police man's shift to end and the next shift will begin in exactly 15 minutes after the first ends. In that 15 minutes they run all the way up the stairs and back into the reception were they run down the left corridor and enter the office on the right, Sheriff Don's office.

They close the door put on the lights to get their quick bearings and switch them off again so as not to draw any attention and then switch on one torch light because two would be harder to handle.

For the next 3 hours they remain locked in his dark office trying to search for clues in the desk drawers, in the cupboards, on the files already on his desk and the mountain of files in the filing cabinet.

They try to hum a little silent hum inside themselves so that the time passes fast and so that they remain calm and forget the possibility of getting caught.

Exactly 3 hours later, they switch on the office lights and that's when they hear a voice and some steps coming down the corridor.

"Hey man what's Sheriff Don's lights doing on at this time of the morning, he almost never stays working that late," said a British accented voice.

As soon as they hear that, they switch the lights off and duck straight into one of the cupboards with the clean shovel that they were arguing about whether to take with them or just leave behind.

Jules turns all pale and Georgie starts to feel sick to his stomach but the feeling subsides as they realize that the Police Officer on duty is too lazy to do his job and so walks in one second and then walks out again the next second.

After that it's all smooth sailing all the way out of the Police Station and back home were Jules stays over and sleeps the night next to me but its safe to say that, that night none of us did any sleeping – we both had our back turned in opposite directions but were just recovering from pulling one of the biggest stunts of our lives.

Of course we came out unscathed and with a bag of clues that needed to be carefully selected and researched without the knowledge of Sheriff Don or our gang, or anybody else for that matter. Some things were left best unsaid and others untold. This is one of them.

## What They Tell The Gang After That Night

"Let's not complicate it Georgie, I will invite them all to a new movie and just as we all gather at the school grounds I will let you do the talking and …"

He interrupts her, "Why me Jules?" he wonders out loud.

"Because you're good with cutting things short, I'm not, it takes me forever to say something when I'm nervous and trying to hide something which we both are doing from them," she explains.

"It's a compliment Georgie," she says.

"Okay consider it a done deal," he says feeling empowered with Jules's words.

The next day as they all gather around in the Common Room on the school grounds, Georgie tells them all that they both talked after the last meeting and decided that it's not worth it to try and get into the Police Station especially when they weren't trying to get hold of one particular things but just entering for the sake of trying to find any clue which they can't guarantee that they will ever find after the break in.

They all looked stunned and they were about to start asking questions and raining down a storm of questions on Georgie when Jules came into his rescue and announced that she's inviting everybody for a movie as her treat and started going on about the fab reviews the movie screening got from critics everywhere, once it first launched in the festival.

# HOW IT ALL FELL INTO PLACE

Once Jason regained his memory, Mr. Whitemore gave the file back to Sheriff Don knowing very well that the file no longer represented a threat to his son's safety and well being.

Sheriff Don's clue that George & Jules found – the muddy foot print truly belonged to Jase and it was the footprint of him taking a shortcut through the woods walking over that (concrete slab – the muddy footprint) on his way to Wilshire Memorial Hospital for help with his mind numbing headache.

Jerry had disappeared in similar circumstances to Jason but unfortunately what appears the same on the outside can in fact be completely different when magnified. Jerry Mac'pheet's body was later discovered two towns over, hidden in a cupboard in the men's toilet at the main Petrol Station in Warrington County on the outskirts of Warrington Hill.

Sheriff Don with his stupidity and lack of training as a Sheriff acted all guilty, held back evidence because he hid away Jason's clue of the muddy footprint afraid that such a clue would land him right smack in the middle of Jason's investigation and hold him wrongly accused and framed. That's what happens when the mayor's son is put to act as the local town's sheriff just because he's his son, contacts can ruin a person's life, they certainly felt like they were ruining his at the time, of course.

Mr. Whitemore and Martha canceled their wedding court date – the 29<sup>th</sup> of April because it brought both of their kinds a lot of agonizing hardships. Teenagers will be teenagers, anxiety and paranoia will remain a constant part of their lives until they reach the sensible age of adulthood. However, years later – they married – I guess what's meant to be will be and time will never get in the way.

George & Jules well – they are like all those teenagers that believe that their first love is their only love until that is, they grow up. A lucky select few, a slim minority, the slimmest of all, get to find out what happens when that first love, years later turns into the only love.

# NOTES